We Truck Louisville

Life Always Needs to Be Protected

We Truck Louisville

Life Always Needs to Be Protected

BEVERLY FEATHERS

ISBN: 978-1-4269-5567-9 (sc)
ISBN: 978-1-4269-5566-2 (e)

Library of Congress Control Number: 2011908483

Trafford rev. 07/18/2011

 www.trafford.com

North America & international
toll-free: 1 888 232 4444 (USA & Canada)
phone: 250 383 6864 ♦ fax: 812 355 4082

Contents

Dedication   WE TRUCK, LOUISVILLE

This is a story of a fantasy battle that did not happen, but was started when the truckers began yelling as they drove through Louisville, Kentucky. This fight was longed for by the truckers, by the police, and by the Louisville Exiles which were terrorized from their homes, along with the other people that fought the mafia takeover of Louisville. These people wanted to push the mafia out, wanted to stop the thieves and burglars from turning the neighborhoods into war zones. When Robert White, Louisville Metro Police Chief, and Irv Maze, Jefferson County Attorney, both came to power, then Louisville surrendered to the tyranny of the mafia terror. The dope dealers had gained control of one more city. –Beverly Feathers

Prologue   WE TRUCK, LOUISVILLE

Bonnie was driving along I64, back to home, when the construction work started to seriously slow down the trip with the stopped jumble of cars. She pulled off on the next exit so that she could drive the back roads through the farm country. Most people would be afraid of this at night. The area was isolated and full of wolves. In the winter the wolves would come closer, drawn to the bright lights in the areas where the people lived. Night jogging in eastern Kentucky cities was not popular because the wolves could just walk through the towns.

She spotted lights just up ahead. Turning off her headlights, she drove slowly to a pull off spot. She walked gingerly to see what was happening. Many people were gagged and tied up, captive on the ground. Some other people were stepping on their throats, using their shoe to hold the heads of the captives steady so that they could brand an "L" on their frightened faces. Bonnie could guess that the "L" was for Louisville, where the great mafia takeover had pushed the landowners off of their property and had impoverished thousands. The "L" would be seen by nobody else because the bodies would disappear. Those were the soon-to-be-dead picks from Louisville. The invaders, the illegal narcotics dealers, that had trained at drug meets, to learn how to rob, swindle, and murder.

She did not turn into a pillar of salt because she had watched those picks being destroyed, like the modern day genocide of a Biblical Sodom and Gomorrah culture. Quietly she walked back to her car. The police had put in the drugs, giving the mafia control of each company in Kentucky. The cops wanted everybody to join the pick so that they would have to pay the dope protection money. Then the picks were treated like ground hamburger. The police would lock up who they wanted and torture who they wanted. Many people had just joined the pick to be safe. But it was only a cycle of abuse. A no win situation with a gang of thieves.

A society would only progress, with people advancing to a better way of life, if there were helpful individuals in a nurturing environment without thieves. Her life and her people had been ruined by the dope gangs. The truckers had yelled in protest of the mafia takeover, when they had driven through Louisville, Kentucky. The drivers had changed their routes so that they could drive through the city and scream, "We truck, Louisville." They wanted the city streets to run red with the blood of the drug dealing invaders.

She took a sip of buttermilk, ate a bite of catfish with cornbread, and then drove on. Bonnie was cold in the freezing weather and wanted to get home to Carl Silas and warmth.

Chapter 1   Dope Takeover

Bonnie was torn between feeling happy and sad today. She was sad about the parts of her life that had been taken from her. But she was also happy because she had found out that there were nice people in the world, too. When she was very young, she had thought that everybody only wanted good things. She had been raised as a Catholic. And she had believed that people were usually mean if they had been hurt a lot, or had misunderstood a tragedy in their lives. Then when she was older, she decided that only a very few people were truly nice. And she was also sad because she could not find more of those nice people.

So she thought about her upside down world. And she relished the lyrics to her favorite song. The words were racing through her mind as she remembered the images of the sadistic Blacks which had pillaged her house each and every day in Louisville, Kentucky. The powerful words, "She went down in a blaze of glory, weapon held tightly in her hand. Body count was in her favor. She had taken every man," gave her support. Bonnie wanted those words close to her right now.

Today she needed to be focused because she was going to hit those cops that were trying to kill her. They were about to get hurt very badly. The only cop that she could almost think nicely about now, was one that she had nicknamed, Winter Hours, because he would push her out of her favorite jogging park earlier during the winter season.

Her thoughts were about how her life was different now. She was no longer living in her strong Catholic community without thieves. Back then, her neighborhood had been full of kids from all the large families. Those kids had been taught not to steal and to treat people with respect. Then the gangs started moving into the area. After forced bussing and desegregation, the value system in the Caucasian culture was threatened.

Suddenly the Blacks had brought a heavy influx of dope and illegal narcotics into her world. That had been very upsetting for the homeowner, Bonnie Plumes. She had been single, gorgeous, athletic, and had liked to dress nice. The Blacks had always been involved with some problem to rob the Caucasians. And because the Blacks were less attractive, they had only wanted to hurt the more pleasant looking white race.

She had bought her clothes at the finer, more expensive stores in completely Caucasian, south Louisville. Bonnie hated it when her clothes had been stolen. She had developed insomnia because of the constant burglaries. Her life was now a battlefield. Instead of finding her one and only love for life, she was avoiding people. Hating all drug dealers, she would never mix with the gangs. The insurmountable obstacle for her to have a married life was the mafia control. There was not anybody to pick for a husband. She just had to fight because circumstances had made the decision for her.

Bonnie had been helping a select few police officers stop the mafia takeover. However, Bert Night of African-American heritage, had been hired as the Louisville Metro Police Chief, so that he could strong arm the mafia into power. And he had swindled everybody with his back stabbing actions and murder attempts. His Black cohorts only wanted to pander dope for the cocaine and heroin market.

The truck drivers had yelled as they drove through Louisville, Kentucky. Those truckers had changed their routes so that they could join the throngs, and scream their protest against the mafia power in the city. The yells went on day and night. The Blacks retaliated to the yelling with their new leader, Bert Night. The police went after the noise and the protesters. So they stopped yelling while their hopes started dwindling. And then the truckers started driving around and avoiding the tyranny of Louisville.

Another thing that happened was that the Federal Bureau of Investigation pulled out of the area. The local offices were only open part of the time. The dope cops were after those F.B.I. files. Kentucky had a problem with faxed information being diverted to many different printers that did not belong to the designated receiver. And with telephone deregulation, the phone service providers could have people listening to phone conversations.

All in all, the lack of security from the dope cops that worked for the organized crime syndicate, created a national safety problem. And it really was a federal offense to establish a network of organized crime. But the cops, along with the bribed county attorneys, wanted the payoff money. So the citizens were terrorized by dope dealers without any recourse for prosecution.

And the truckers decided to refuse to accept Louisville, Kentucky loads and deliveries. The cops were handing out false traffic tickets and false warrants. The drug dealers were told to get false warrants placed on the people that they wanted to rob. The drug rats had taken over the city with thefts and terrorism. And the police were fighting for the drug payoff money.

Now the lazy cops were barking for more burglaries and false imprisonments. The west end of Louisville was always the center of the scum world. And the west end gangs mercilessly robbed the south end. The stores were robbed of merchandise and cash. The managers just took the money from the cash registers so that the businesses would close. Gas stations would quickly change from Quicky Gas to Fuel Tiger, because the stations were sold. Then the stations would change again from Fuel Tiger to Gas Now, as all the money was taken by the managers, and the stations were sold again.

And the Caucasians that mixed with the Blacks in the west end were just as bad as the Black gang members. The neighborhoods and city blocks were populated with whites or blacks, only. Any mixed housing area was only a place that was going to be Black in the future, as the whites were pushed out. The Blacks, which were predators, would always push the Caucasians out. The racial segregation laws were in place for years because the Blacks can not peacefully coexist with another race. They are predators.

Bonnie was always ironically amused by the Supreme Court ruling to desegregate. The findings of the judges were that the Blacks could learn and be taught, and were therefore not inferior. The fact that the Blacks would only rob, loot, and pillage the Caucasian neighborhoods was not addressed. So the predators were let loose on the white communities with the court order to desegregate. The Black culture operated with the premise that theft, swindling, and burglaries were a required social custom. Those Blacks believed that burglaries were mandatory necessities, like food and water. Bonnie believed that predators were inferior and self-destructive.

Knowing that a society would only progress if there were not thieves to hold back development, Bonnie wondered at that blunder in Supreme Court judgment. If people had to repeatedly buy the same thing over and over again because they had been robbed, then they could not use their income for any new things. The thieves would just keep topple advancement while their victims would never get ahead.

In college, she had tried to avoid any classes with African studies. Apparently, so had everybody else because those courses were the ones that were usually left open for registration. When there had been only one open class for a required course, she was forced to take a class that covered African tribesmen. According to the material, Africa was hot during the day and near freezing at night. The tribesmen wandered in nomadic disarray and gathered wild growing food, like nuts and berries.

There was a stark void with the lack of investigative research and invention by the tribesmen. They did not progress to a higher technological state independently. Bonnie was not taught that the tribesmen wrote great musical compositions, epic novels, or highly emotional poems. What she was told was that the tribes just existed in a barbaric state. The Africans were primitive and showed no intention of wanting to live in a more civilized way.

So the White Man's Burden for progress was shown to Bonnie very clearly by her courses. The Caucasians had to develop industry, language, and science so that there would be roadways and electricity. And Bonnie knew that the gangs would destroy that progress. That destruction would be a result of the social impact of slavery. The Blacks had been captured and brought to this country. Slavery had immigrated thousands of Blacks that would have never been able to afford travel to the United States.

All those slaves had been in the homes of the slave owners. The slaves had cooked the food, had washed the clothes, and had cleaned the homes. The idea that the slave owners had eaten food that was cooked by the slaves was always surprising to Bonnie. That food probably contained very disgusting things that were put in it by the slaves. She knew that she could never have been able to have slept in a house with slaves, much less eat the food that had been cooked by the slaves. The slaves had been captured and would have only hurt their captors.

So now she was being attacked by gangs that were made up of the descendants of slaves, and lower class Caucasians. She was terrorized by a predatory group of drug dealers. And fighting a war against them, had put her in places and caused actions, that had not even been considered by her when she had been growing up as a gracious southern belle. She had become an aggressive, pioneering warrior that was fighting dope dealers.

All those things that she remembered, had forced Bonnie to take a stand. Pushing those thoughts away for a moment, she looked around at the passing buildings and streets, so that she could watch for any danger. In her battle role, Bonnie was now driving a Polito fuel tanker, with king size bed pillows stuffed under her clothes for padding. She was steering the fuel tanker toward the Louisville Police Station on Jefferson Street.

She had killed the Polito driver, Doug Thomas, and stole the tanker. Doug had been crime syndicate, drug dealing vermin. That was an easy kill for her because she liked to kill all dope dealers. Now she had to slow down, so that she could roll off the tractor onto the pavement. She was standing with the tractor door open as she watched the usual landmarks of her home town slide past. And she would blow up their police station with great pleasure.

She wanted to see the flames burst through the windows after her Polito tanker exploded the building. Bonnie longed to see their mangled bodies because those cops had robbed and murdered her people. But she could not wait around. She needed to run away before she was caught. She had been in that police building a couple of hundred times and wanted to watch it crumble. Their deaths would not be enough in exchange for the murdered friends and other people that she knew had been killed by the drug gangs that had been put in by Bert Night. Those disgusting gangs were told to kill anyone that would not sell illegal narcotics.

So Bonnie rolled off the tractor, and bounced up to run fast and hard. She could face a terrible penalty for this little police roaster maneuver. The despot county attorneys and dope dealing cops would make her final years a nightmare. The blast was loud as the flames brought light to the darkness. Strangely, no one was screaming. Then she heard the yells. The pavement felt like glue sticking to her shoes as she thought about being caught. She ran faster with the cold fear of sweat covering her.

Being caught was not an option for her. Bonnie fought back the fear and dread that was deep inside her, as she took each of her running steps. Cold numbing fright almost paralyzed her. She focused ahead with no conscious thought for losing. Her intelligence told her that losing was possible, that she was only playing the odds. Bonnie had her muscled, athletic body for a winning edge. But the fear was still there. Then she was finally safe, across the river, in Indiana. Kentucky had suffered another blow in her fight for freedom against the drug lord tyrants.

She stopped to look around for just a few seconds, remembering the bridge. Only a few days before, a trucker had stolen a rig from Belons Trucking, and had hit one of the Louisville Metro Police cruisers on that I65, Indiana to Kentucky bridge, at a speed of more than 50 miles per hour. The truckers hated the Louisville cops that were blocking the traffic lanes on the bridge.

The police car had bounced onto another car, and sailed over the bridge railing. The doors had been crushed. And the windows had been shattered. With the lights and siren running, the police car had whimpered to a tiny whine below the Ohio River, just seconds after the police officer had jumped through the open car window into the cold river water. The cruiser took the cop down with the undertow. He was still missing. And the truckers wanted him dead.

Bert Night had been sending police officers to kill Bonnie outside of Jefferson County so that he could avoid being charged with her murder. Only two nights ago, in Shelby County, a Louisville police officer was already running his lights and siren from Exit 35 on I64 as Bonnie, heading east, had passed below the overpass. She turned on the radio when she saw the cruiser chasing from behind her. In the dark, she could plainly see the Louisville police car.

She pulled her Jeep over to the emergency lane. The officer walked to the back of her car as if to check her license plate. Bonnie saw the gun in his hand as he yelled for her to turn off the car. She put the car in reverse and ran over the cop. Then she drove over him again as she used her rear tire to crush his head. She had a dead cop under her car. But Bonnie had altered her license plate numbers. So now the cops would only be looking for her kind of car, not her car exactly, if they even cared enough to search.

And one week before that, Josh Toucan, a St. Matthews police officer had tried to kill her in Jefferson County. All the county attorneys were ignoring the corrupt police attacks because they were lounging back on their mafia payoff money. Toucan was deformed and slow witted, like the rest of his ilk. Dope cops were obese misfits, obnoxious social rejects, and very dangerous. They made more with payoff money than they could make just working as police officers. But they also had to kill people. And that was a perk, instead of a downside, to those loser badges. Dirty dope cops enjoyed killing.

She just wanted to vomit when one of them spoke to her. And Bonnie always informed the Federal Bureau of Investigation when one of the dope cops tried to kill her. She had simply driven away from Jefferson County while Toucan was smirking in front of a crowd of witnesses. With the people watching, he had grimaced like a child that had been caught trying to sneak a cookie from a cookie jar. Toucan had backed off, stepped away from her, and got in his car. She used that opportunity, with a little luck, to leave Jefferson County very quickly, before Toucan got a second idea about how to kill her.

That was the kind of abuse that the truckers had been fighting against for a very long time. The battle cry, "We truck, Louisville," was all that remained of the yelling that the drivers had used to hit Louisville, Kentucky when the mafia had first taken over the city. The shouting was in the past, now. And the drivers no longer intentionally changed their routes to drive through the city and yell.

They and others had just yelled different things as they had driven along the streets in Louisville. Mostly, the yelling was about something that had happened unfairly. The yells could be the name of a vile cop or a bad business. The shouts might be, "Mait," or "Night," or, could even be, "school board." The protest was like the Boston Tea Party because the people opposed tyranny and social injustice.

"Mait" and "Night" were common yells. Earl Mait was the Jefferson County Attorney. And Bert Night was the Louisville Police Chief. Both of them were famous for false prosecution. False warrants and false charges went together with the same group of witnesses. The Louisville police would simply write a false traffic ticket. Then the court system would prosecute the falsely accused.

Anybody could face false criminal charges. Dope dealers were like toys for the dope cops. The drug dealers would hit and attack for the payoff cops. Then, depending on the whim of the dirty cop, that same dope dealer could be killed or locked up in prison. The illegal narcotics network was an endless cycle of abuse with a no win outcome. Paying protection money and joining gangs would not make anybody safe. And even if people had already known that, the money hungry payoff cops would still be able to force them into the dope gangs for the sport of torture.

With all of this happening, people would just avoid the city while Louisville, Kentucky inanely tried to promote tourism. The place was like a spider web, waiting to catch the unsuspecting. There was a huge Louisville Slugger bat in the city, on the outside of a downtown building, and as tall as a building, that was supposed to attract visitors. But the thieves in the city were too much. You could just eat a hard boiled egg, look at the large Louisville Slugger Bat from a tour bus seat, and pretend to have taken a trip, just to be on the safe side. Southern hospitality was not to be found in that town anymore.

The rumor was that the crime syndicate came from the Chicago, Illinois mafia. Truckers would not even stop overnight in Chicago. They would park outside the city, drive in with their loads, and then leave. None of the truckers would wait in Chicago for a business to open so that the driver could unload a trailer. The truckers definitely did not want another Chicago scenario. Any kind of damage could happen in Chicago.

Louisville, Kentucky damage would include false tickets, false warrants, and false imprisonments that accompanied the rule of corrupt Jefferson County Attorney, Earl Mait. The police were told to arrest anybody that they did not want and to divide that person's personal property among the drug dealers. In response, the truckers were intelligently refusing to accept any Louisville loads and avoiding the city. So the war had shifted into a different arena with covert attacks against the tyranny of the mafia and the bribed officials.

And the drug dealers, the invaders that had been told to get false warrants on people that they did not want, were gloating. The police would get the false warrants pushed through for the dope dealers. So after you had been robbed, and your property had been vandalized each day, you would find yourself in court facing false charges with lying witnesses that only wanted to steal the rest of what you owned.

Polite southern people that had raised their kids so that they would not steal, had tremendous difficulty coping with the complete lack of integrity and relentless thefts. The kids would hopelessly respond to the gang pressure in the schools. So they would ultimately join a gang and end up robbing their parents. Moms and dads looking for thieves, would not suspect their children. The biggest shock would be when the kids would try to kill their own parents.

And the Blacks had terrorized the Caucasian neighborhoods to the Bullitt County line. Like African tribes, the Blacks would walk through the yards, trampling the gardens where the families had been growing vegetables to make summer favorites, like bacon, lettuce, and tomato sandwiches with watermelons. Now, their lives were destroyed by gang violence. And their lives were only protected by the muscles in their body and the battle cry, "We truck, Louisville."

That war cry had brought Bonnie this far. Bonnie leaned against her car for a few seconds so that she could get her keys out of her zippered pocket. Then she unlocked her car and turned on the tiny battery operated television. The car was warming up. She stared at herself in the rear view mirror. There she was, waiting for the car to reach operating temperature as she watched the television for the reports on the police station that she had just blown up. Bonnie was not going to drive that car away with a cold engine unless there was a threat.

When the car was ready, there was still no news report to guide her choice of direction. So she took the back roads north into Indiana and crossed back into Kentucky at the bridge near Madison. Frankfort was a regular place for her to be. Therefore, picking up I64 at the Versailles Road exit would not attract attention to her. She drove hard, but casually into eastern Kentucky.

Then the news reports were mostly about the police officers that had been burned alive. She wanted to see pictures of the burned and mangled cops. But there was only live coverage of the building that showed how part of the police station had landed on Seventh Street, blocking the driving lanes. Bonnie turned the television off. She was very far away from that problem now. There were not going to be any road blocks to stop her on her way home.

The generally accepted response for most people, was to stay out of Louisville, Kentucky and not to help the city. People were afraid of the thieves that lived there. Even the Kentucky State Police did not want to patrol the city. There was not a Kentucky State Police post in Jefferson county. And, apparently the state police were not too concerned with an attack on the Louisville police because there no roadblocks. So she could just drive peacefully away from the battlefield.

Bonnie was still pumped up when she turned into her driveway. Her home was quiet. She went to run a hot bath and toss her clothes in the washer. When she had killed Doug Thomas, next to his Polito tanker, there had not been any blood. So she could just wash her clothes. She had worn common, everyday black sweats with a black hooded jacket. She hoped that if anybody had seen her, that they would not know that she was a woman. Mostly, she hoped that nobody had seen anything. Especially, she sincerely wished, that not one person had even been able to connect any woman with the fuel tanker attack.

Bonnie did not want to be charged. She did not feel like a criminal. Fighting for freedom against tyranny, she only felt a burning hate for the organized crime syndicate. She knew that torturing and robbing people was wrong even if the police departments were encouraging the sadistic behavior. The entire system was corrupt.

So she fought. And being tall was something that had worked for her when she killed somebody. A short person may have difficulty passing themself off as a man. Bonnie could bulk up with stuffing and look like a big man. The problem was that she knew that she had to fight and that she could not win. Realistically, the most that they could do was to keep the corruption out of safe areas. She was going to push the dope dealers away, back into their county.

As she soaked in the grapefruit scented bubble bath, she thought about how futile her time would be if she were caught. The mafia was not going to just say never mind, take back the city, keep the protection racket money, and whine that the fighting was too much. She knew that the crime syndicate was easier to keep out than to put out. Preventing a mafia takeover, like preventing cancer, was much simpler than pushing the mafia out and curing cancer.

She knew that Louisville, Kentucky had the manpower and resources to keep out the takeover that Bonnie was risking her life to stop. But Louisville had changed sides in the fight when they began supporting the mafia with the Black push for drug power and gangs. She was just going to draw a line and fight the enemy back, behind the line. Keep the thieves out with segregated, crime free areas.

And she did not understand why the lesser intelligent people formed gangs. The country had experienced forced bussing. The minorities had only turned the Caucasian neighborhoods into crime ridden, gang controlled, places. The gang mentality of the lower class had moved into the middle economic class. The thefts by the lower class poor people had bankrupted the investments of the middle class people because they had been wiped out by the thieves. Those economic losses trickled into the corporations. The result was the low interest rates on the savings accounts in the banks.

People with house payments for $400,000 homes were suddenly unemployed because the mafia only wanted the dope dealers to be employed in the companies. The foreclosures and defaulted loans had created credit problems for homeowners that would last a lifetime. Instead of wondering which university to choose for their children, they were wondering why they were unexpectedly impoverished.

The illegal narcotics dealers gave out illegal keys to houses and cars. They copied every key that they got from their dope dealers. Night office cleaning businesses had lots of keys to copy. People had their personal account information illegally given out to the dope dealers. The drug dealers had files on everybody. And burglarizing homes, combined with reporting each new purchase in a store, kept track of everything that the victims had owned and had bought. Cars and homes were vandalized.

Therefore, putting tapeworms in the food was an easy way for the dope dealers to infect people. And Bonnie had serious trouble with the tapeworms. She did not eat out in restaurants anymore. The tapeworms were put in her refrigerator food while her neighbors had used the illegal key that they had to her house. She had back pain and a generally lousy feeling because of the tapeworm infection.

Her neighbors, Danny and Marcella Duff, were real nut cases that drove all over her property when she was not at home. Bonnie had bought a truck when she had started remodeling her house. So then, Danny Duff bought a truck. And he would walk over and vandalize Bonnie's truck. Marcella Duff would come over and cut branches off of Bonnie's trees. The roses that Bonnie had planted were doused with chlorine bleach by Marcella.

Bonnie was such a nice, polite, recycling kind of person, that she did not find out how evil the Duffs were for a long time. It was so completely unthinkable to Bonnie that people would act that way. But the situation became much worse when Marcella Duff wanted to build a carport on Bonnie's side yard. Bonnie would not sign over permission. So the Duffs conspired with some of Bonnie's relatives to have Bonnie killed for life insurance.

She had moved forward from that murder attempt realization to blowing up a police station. Bonnie stopped thinking about the past and started focusing on the future. She had decided to listen to all the news about her police station bombing so that she would know all the facts. Bonnie was supposed to have not been anywhere near Louisville, Kentucky at the time of the bombing. She thought that blowing up a police station was a very mild response to the terrorism. Bonnie knew that all those dope gang members had agreed to rob and murder anybody that did not sell drugs.

That was why her muscles were still tense after almost two hours in the hot, bubbly water. She was livid and in pain. Her back was better today. And the heat would always ease the pain a little more. The tapeworms had done a lot of damage with the infection. Poisoning and infecting people were just a few of the things that the drug dealers were taught to do at their drug meets. And Bonnie just clenched and unclenched her fists as her rage raced higher because of the damage to her body. She muttered with vibrant distaste, "Such a foul thing to do to a person with so much potential."

She had held onto great dreams early in her life. Bonnie wanted to be a doctor and knew that she needed to be trusted by people. When she went to high school, she had just picked some people to be her friends so that she would not be labeled a freak and a loner. Bonnie followed social convention. And she did not even like her high school friends. She thought about how she had just quickly picked some people to be her friends in high school and about how she really still did not have any true, close friends now.

Her best friend was supposed to be Elizabeth Hempson. That was a sad situation. Beth Hempson was a loser. When Beth got a job at Burger Dome, she had her parents co-sign a car loan for her. Then Beth just decided to quit her job with a petty little whine about being told to do too much by a mean and nasty boss. And she fixed that problem by writing some stupid letters to the loan company to tell them that she was looking for a job, and to ask them to wait for the payments. Her parents just started making her car payments for her so that they could protect their credit rating after the loan company sent them a collection letter for the car payments.

And Beth would steal anything. She was so irresponsible that she did not even have a locking gas cap on her car. So naturally, someone stole the gas cap off of Beth's car. Being a total loser, she decided to scout around a parking lot to find a car like hers. And then, she savagely stole a gas cap from another car on the parking lot. Buying a locking gas cap never was a choice that would be considered by her.

So Bonnie had these friends to help her keep up an appearance for a normal teenage life. Hating thieves, she quickly relegated Beth to a for-show-only acquaintance. Beth would ask Bonnie to go places with her. And Bonnie would say that she was too busy with schoolwork or whatever. Then Beth would show up anyway to pick Bonnie up. After a few words between them, in front of Bonnie's mom, Bonnie would just leave with Beth and wonder if they were going to be killed or hold up a store.

And if high school was bad, college was a worse time for Beth. Bonnie really tried to avoid Beth on campus. Beth was not lacking in college dysfunctional behavior. Bonnie bought a parking permit for her car. And Beth did not buy a parking permit for her car. However, Beth still parked on campus. Beth would casually throw away all her university parking tickets.

So one day, Beth telephoned to report that her car had been stolen. When the campus police came to take the report, the officer found out that Beth's car had been towed away by the campus police and had been impounded because of the unpaid parking tickets. The campus cop said, "You did not pay your parking tickets. So your car was towed away. The tickets total more than one hundred dollars."

And with Beth's usual lack of resourcefulness, she told the officer that she did not have any money. Beth whined, "I never got any parking tickets on my car. And I do not have any money with me. Especially not one hundred dollars."

The officer told her, "There is not a campus permit registered to your car. You need a permit to park in this lot. And your car will not be released, you will not receive your grades, until you pay for the tickets and the other charges."

Beth was really angered by that information. They were going to keep her car. She seethed, and argued, "I need my car to get home. I can get the money and pay for everything tomorrow. I have to study for a test. You know that I will be here for an exam. Why don't you just drive me to my car? I will fix everything tomorrow."

"You can not just pick up your car. You have to pay first. Tickets were left on your car. And even if somebody just took the tickets off, you still should have known, with all those posted signs, that you needed a campus permit to park here," the officer told her.

Beth would not give up, and said, "I need to get home, somehow. I need my car."

"I can give you a ride to the campus police station so that you can call somebody for a ride home," the cop responded to her before he answered a police radio call.

Then Beth did give up. She was afraid that they might lock up her if she went to the campus police station. She just looked around and told the cop, "No. Never mind. I see a friend of mine over there. I need to hurry to catch them. I have to go. Now." And she raced away. She went to wait for Bonnie in the Chemical Engineering Building.

Bonnie just stared at Beth when she saw her standing there, in the hallway, after the chemistry class. Bad news Beth was looking very sad. She just snapped at Bonnie, "The cops towed my car away. I need over a hundred dollars to get my car back. They said that I had parking tickets. Somebody must have taken the tickets off of my car. I need to get my car today so that I can study for a test. The campus police officer told me that I could use their phone to call for a ride. But I was afraid that they would lock me up."

"Beth, you told me that you threw the parking tickets away, remember? And you said that you were not going to spend any money on a campus parking permit. You must be in shock if you can just lie to me like that. Do you really think that I believe your sad stuff? I can not give you my money for another one of your lamed brain stunts," Bonnie said. Then Bonnie started pacing in the hallway.

"The police should have put you in jail and not your tiny car. That car is just a victim of abuse. You would not even feed your kids if you had any. You are a worthless, stupid person. You will never do anything right. And, just let me guess. Now you want me to take you home. Okay. Come on. Now, we go. Your dad will be home in an hour. He will take care of it," Bonnie offered to her.

"I need my car! They can not just take my car," Beth whimpered. "Your parents are making the payments on your car. None of your stories will work on me. You are a disaster. And now, you have had your innocent little car locked up. You did not take of the car. Beth, you never take care of anything. In high school, we hung around, went to pep rallies, and joined a lot of science fiction clubs. That is over. I am trying to get into medical school now. I grew up. You are holding me back. If I try to use you for a reference, they are just going to tell me that your parole board intercepted the letter of recommendation from you," Bonnie blurted out.

Beth retaliated with, "My car! Mine!"

"Shut up, you whiner. Trouble, trouble is all that you are. You hurt your car. You are hurting me. I have to study for classes, too. Now just walk quickly with me to my car. And put up your jacket hood. Put on your sunglasses so that people will not recognize you with me. If I had some scissors, I would just cut off your hair for a better disguise. Probably, shave your head," Bonnie ordered.

Beth just stopped walking. She told Bonnie, "You have enough money with you to get my car out of the car prison."

"Oh, no. That will not happen. I will not give you the money. Remember when we went to Florida, after high school, and you ran out of money. We were eating at that Chinese buffet restaurant. And you just looked at me with those pathetic eyes. You said that you could not pay for your lunch. I had to drive the whole way to Florida. You were reading the map. You directed me to a street that was a dead end into the ocean," Bonnie informed her. She stared directly into Beth's face. Beth kept her innocent and angry expression.

"Then, you just threw the street map on the back seat and stared at me. I was staring at the ocean. And I wanted to know how to get to the street for our hotel. You did not help me. I had to drive and find my way out. Then, I had to pay your way for most of the time that we were in Florida. If I was going to pay, at least I could have been paying for a guy to go with me. You only gave me my money back after we got home. I wanted to spend my money, on me, in Florida. I wanted to shop in Atlanta, Georgia on the way back. But you used my money in Florida," Bonnie barked.

She turned around the hall corner while Beth started following her again. "I will not give you any more money. I have patients that want to see me in the future when I am a doctor. You are a goof off. We are going to ask your dad for the money before your mother, the rule maker of pain, gets home. So hurry up, a lot faster than that. Short, Caucasian girls with long brown hair, like you, can walk fast, too," Bonnie whispered to her.

They were next to Bonnie's car, when Beth said, "You ask my dad for the money. I am wiped out from all of this."

"Did you completely drain out all of your brain cells? You are just afraid. And when I told you that your dad walked up and kissed me on the neck, when I stayed the weekend with you, back in high school, I clearly intended not to intercede for you with him again. Your mom would throw me out of your house and keep me out. My parents should never be told anything like that. The words Catholic convent would come up. I was just walking out from a shower, in your bathrobe, and he kissed me on the neck. I do not need any kind of social label or problem to block me from medical school just because your dad kissed me. You have to ask him," Bonnie advised her.

Beth's dad made her wait one week for the money. Bonnie had to take her to campus each day. So they just started stopping each day for food at a restaurant or at the mall. Bonnie had received some gift cards for Christmas presents, so she bought lunch for two. The two of them talked about all their troubles. Beth started relaxing more because of those shopping trips. And Bonnie gave her an early birthday present, when Beth wanted a sweater in the Tops Priced store. The gift cards were handy for that week. Bonnie would probably have just used the gift cards by eating alone in a restaurant with a textbook. Today she would never eat in a restaurant.

She had not seen Beth in many years. Bonnie had only needed to have friends in high school so that she would not look like a freak. She did not go to any high school reunions. She had herself listed as not available to be reached for high school alumni events.

Beth's dad had told Bonnie, when she had seen him, some time ago, in a store, that Beth had finally been pawned off to some divorced guy as his second wife. Her dad said that they did not have Bonnie's new address and telephone number, so that was why she was never invited to the wedding.

Bonnie had looked at him and said, "Beth needs to spend time with her new husband and not with me. I had too many harassing phone calls and got an unlisted number. And besides, your wife would have exploded if she knew that you kissed me when I was a teenager. My parents would have been after you for that, too. I did not need those kinds of problems in high school. Having people talk about me kissing my best friend's dad, would have not been great for me. And that is how the talk would have turned out. I would have been labeled a tramp. You did a vile thing when you kissed me on the neck. You are a wimpy little person on the inside."

Beth's dad, James, looked horrified and asked, "Does my wife know?"

"I told Beth about it just after you did that. I walked into her bedroom and said that you had kissed me on the neck. Her eyes filled with tears. I told her that we should not tell her mom or my parents. Things would just get bad for me. I was going to attend medical school. You are a filthy pig for treating people like that. If I was your wife, I would have divorced you because you kissed one of your daughter's sixteen year old friends. You did not get away without any consequences. Your daughter knew. And she does like to gossip. I just did not need that kind of scandal," Bonnie told him. Then she just walked away from him.

James stood near the check out lane cash register when Bonnie bought her things. She just glanced back at him before she left the store. He had the nerve to wave good-bye to her. Bonnie just kept walking to her car. Then James left the store to follow her. He was not her dad. James was only about eighteen years older than Bonnie. He walked up beside her, next to her car. James looked at her and said, "I want to call you."

"We do not have any reason to talk. I remember how your wife, Page, would come in the back door while we were all watching the television. She would yell about why the dishes were not washed, why the kitchen was not cleaned, and why the house was a mess. I just wanted to hide under the sofa pillows, then. I would not have liked to have heard her call me a dirty little tramp. You do not have any reason to call me," Bonnie answered.

James replied, "We could go out. You are not a kid anymore, Bonnie. You are a grown, beautiful woman. I would like to have a second wife." He just laughed and his blue eyes sparkled with fun.

"We are not going out. My telephone number is unlisted for a reason. Right now, the only thing, hat I want to do is to tell Beth, that now her dad has just asked me out for a date after that long ago kiss. But I am not going to call Beth. We have lost touch for a long time. Beth was an irresponsible person that became a burden to me. Now I am leaving. There is a woman, over there that is listening to us. I need to go. And do not follow me, James," Bonnie instructed him.

James looked at her, and said, "A long time ago I came to your house. You told me that you were going to be home that night. When I pulled onto your driveway, all the house lights were off. Your car was there. You must have been asleep. I tossed an empty beer can on your front lawn. And I am not afraid to tell anyone that I, Charles Barker, want to marry you."

"I remember that beer can. I did not want your trashy beer can on my front yard," Bonnie replied. Then she laughed out loud until her smile faded.

Softly, she whispered, "Your name is James Hempson, not Charles Barker. And you appear to be very experienced with sneaking around on your wife."

He just smiled and whispered, "I did not want to be caught with an empty beer can in my car. Your trash can was probably on the back porch. I did not want to creep around your property."

"Now you have used a correct word. Creep describes you perfectly. You were just angry and tossed the can at my yard. I was never afraid of you. But you place me in an unfavorable position. Page would never be nice to me again. And I have done nothing to create a problem. You would have enjoyed yourself roaming around my yard. However, my neighbors would have telephoned Page as soon as they saw you. So you would have went home to a very informed wife," Bonnie said.

James stepped away from her car. Then he stepped forward to help her close the car door after she got in. He waved again. And he said, "You know that I am a great guy. Be careful, Bonnie," as she drove away.

Bonnie had thought about Page as she had driven home that day. If Page had called her a tramp, that would have embarrassed Bonnie. The whole scandal would have been nauseating for Bonnie, too. And Bonnie would have been in trouble with her parents back then, just because James had kissed her. A very bad situation had been caused by that smiling, smirking man with blue eyes that had helped her a few times when she had been a teenager.

Yes, she would have been embarrassed to have had to deal with that problem. But she was not embarrassed by blowing up the police station or by ruthlessly killing dope dealers. Bonnie did hate and kill all illegal narcotics dealers with her own intense lust for justice and vengeance. And she was extremely proud of her hate for thieves, sadists, and torturers.

Bonnie thought her other fight, her ongoing battle to get rid of the effects of the tapeworm infection. Her intestines had sores and growths that she needed to remove without surgery. Her natural medicines were helping. But she still needed to see another physician so that she could keep herself free of the parasites.

She ate pumpkin seeds, garlic, grapefruit seed extract, and used bromelain. Bonnie had read about bromelain at the health food store. The enzyme, bromelain, was in fresh pineapple. All the information that she found on bromelain reported that it would actually destroy tapeworms. So she used these natural medicines to expel and kill tapeworms. But she also needed to heal her intestines.

When she had first noticed a difference in her health, she had tried to decide what the problem was doing to her. While she was reading about her symptoms, she came across information about tapeworm and hookworm infections. Then she tried some bromelain with pumpkin seeds. That did something to help. Her abdomen had actually moved inward when the tapeworms had left.

The whole feeling was like the tapeworms had been pressing against her intestines. It was as if they had been pushing hard, in the same way that a person would push with their feet against the footboard of a bed. And they were crowded, too. Bonnie expelled at least seventy of those pale, dull white parasites at one time.

Then she went to see a doctor for a prescription. Mebendazole, albendazole, and praziquantel were usually prescribed. Bonnie used a prescription for albendazole. And she followed up her treatment with the natural medicines. Her back pain was not so bad anymore. The tapeworms had given her a lot of discomfort. But she had used heat and sports rubs with methyl salicylate to ease the pain. Steamy hot baths had helped immensely.

And tomorrow she had an appointment with Dr. Blake. Carl Silas Blake, M.D. would tell her if the tapeworms were gone. The office should have the test results ready. Bonnie needed to be there early. She also wanted to get another prescription for amoxicillin so that she could control the effects of the infection.

Natural medicines were good. But the prescriptions were stronger and more effective. Poliomyelitis was no longer such a problem because there were vaccines available to control polio. And Bonnie treated the tapeworm infection with the same seriousness as polio. She wanted anything that she could get to help her. Tomorrow, she would allow lots of time for questions at the doctor's office.

But she was tired now and wanted to go sleep. And Bonnie doubted that she would have any nightmares about the exploding police station. She never had bad dreams about killing dope dealers. There would just be this relaxed feeling with a sense of accomplishment after she had killed a drug dealer. She would only feel that part of her very big job was done. So she just brushed a coconut oil conditioner through her hair and went to sleep.

Chapter 2   Married

That appointment had been a long time ago. Now she was hurrying home to Carl Silas Blake. Things had changed like a roller coaster ride. Bonnie just bounced and tumbled her way along. The dope gangs had taken the rhyme and reason out of her life. She felt like a daughter of the American Revolution, or a survivor from the American Civil War. Her choices were calculated with survival instincts, not with pleasure or desire.

Carl Silas was standing inside the front door when Bonnie got home. She always made sure that he did not come home to an empty house. Last night she had made dinner for his friends from college. The medical school crowd only had to microwave the dinner of steaks, tomato salad, white cheddar potato slices, fresh baked flax seed bread, green beans with onions, and German chocolate cake. And there were plenty of potato chips and other snacks.

She would have felt out of place with those people. Bonnie was not jealous and did not have any time to be jealous. She was not going to hang around that dinner just see if any of his previous girlfriends showed up. And she did not even ask about his girlfriends. The idea of other girlfriends was not important to her. Carl Silas had just wanted to be married. And she had married him when he had asked her. She had agreed to be married and started coming home to him so that he would have a wife.

But tonight, she was late. That made him alone for those few hours. She was hoping that he would stay at the hospital a little longer. But he had come straight home. So Bonnie had to make him satisfied and pampered again. She cooked the chicken, fixed a salad, and poured the orange juice. She asked him about his day and asked him if he needed anything. Bonnie tried to squeeze tightly inside his thoughts, so that he would feel wanted by her and not alone. She asked him if he would take the cornbread out of the oven in about twenty minutes while she took a quick shower. Bonnie always ask him because she always did things his way.

She did not like the fact that he thought he that had to make up excuses when he did something that he wanted. He did not have to tell her everything. And he did not have to tell her his false story alibis, either. She just wanted him to let it go. He would be gone, but not dead, and come back. But tonight he might ask her about her time. He never cared about her interests. And he did not have to care. She took care of things. Bonnie was content with the arrangement.

They ate dinner quietly. Bonnie did not want to trigger any searching questions. He had talked with his friends last night in private. She had thought that privacy was for the best while he was with his friends last night. She asked him if tonight's dinner was okay. If he did not like it, she would quickly make something else. He was pampered and spoiled by being given everything that he wanted.

She had told him to give his friends all the food that was not eaten from his dinner last night. Let his friends take any leftover food home with them. Never mind any fuss with bowls, because she had put everything on disposable party keeper food trays.

She knew that she would only sleep a few hours tonight. Bonnie liked to curl up next to his tall, muscular body. Hardly moving while she was asleep, she would not wake him.

At the time when her nightmares had started again, then he had quickly opened his eyes from sleep. He would mutter, "What happened?" She would place her hand over his mouth before he launched into a complete attack, as if wild Indians had invaded the homestead. Even her slight movements would bring him wide awake. She usually would press tightly against his chest, under his arm, absorbing his heat. Bonnie was always tired and cold.

She knew that he was content when they both went to sleep. At about three o'clock in the morning, she woke up and slipped from the bed. Bonnie soaked in a hot, bubble bath until about six o'clock in the morning. Then she got dressed and made the breakfast that Carl Silas had requested last night. Always, she gave him what he wanted, and so easily. He ate breakfast while she talked about trying to increase her jogging distance. Bonnie only wanted her hot herbal tea for breakfast this morning. She was languid after her long soak. When her husband left for the hospital, she started her morning jog. Bonnie ate some fresh pineapple with cashews while she cooled down after her run. Then she finished the rest of her morning exercises and thought about the past again.

Fresh pineapple was often something that she used for a three day fast, since she had been infected with hookworms. Bonnie tried to keep garlic, pumpkin seeds, and bromelain, the enzyme from fresh pineapple, in her diet. None of those things had an unpleasant taste. And, they would also help get rid of tapeworms. But some of the natural medicines that she had tried would make her gag from the foul taste.

That was the problem with grapefruit seed extract. So Bonnie would put drops of the extract in empty gelatin capsules from the health food store. When she had tried wormwood, she had started using the slide apart capsules. Bonnie would use an eyedropper to let the drops of tincture fall into the capsules before she would slide them together again. Wormwood and grapefruit seed extract did not taste good.

Mostly, she liked to use the bromelain tablets from the health food store. Natural medicines, to get rid of hookworms and tapeworms, were good to have when she could not continuously use the prescriptions for albendazole, mebendazole, or praziquantel. Those worm parasites had done some serious damage by making sores on her intestines. Her back had hurt and her joints had swollen from the infection. She was uncomfortable when she stood on her feet for more than a few hours. Sitting in a chair was much better.

Tapeworms, in food, were part of the drug traffic problem. Hurting people, stealing things, and tearing things up were the only things that she could see from that kind of lifestyle. She had been terrorized, almost killed, and nearly wiped out by dope dealers. And they could not care less. Drug dealers were selfish and superficial maggots that fed on the accomplishments of others. She would buy something. And then they would steal what she had just bought. Dope dealers were a threat that she needed to make go away.

But the illegal narcotics network just continued to grow. She knew that Joe Aaronson, the Louisville mayor, would be looking for a another drug dealing police chief, when Bert Night was gone. The mayor of Louisville liked to use dope. The entire situation was caustic. Bonnie's people would need to stymie efforts for any new police chief. With no police chief on staff, Louisville would be even less threatening. Intercepting applications and eliminating candidates would be a good stall.

The mafia had taken over Louisville, Kentucky and was not going to simply leave. Keeping the mafia out in the first place, was her choice of action for the area. And Louisville had been large enough to stop a mafia takeover, if the power people had been against it. The police had rolled and barked like dogs after a bone, so that they could collect that drug payoff money.

And because of that, tapeworms had hurt her health, damaged her body. Bonnie liked to stay in shape. And she liked that her natural beauty routine was intense, but not surgical. She was going to keep looking good, being good, with or without Carl Silas in her life. Bonnie would peel away layers of dead skin so that she would not have a dead skin buildup to form wrinkles. Calcium bentonite clay mask was her favorite for sloughing off dead skin. The clay would dry and crack while it pulled her face tight, until she scrubbed it off.

She always wanted to look good for the other part of her life, her dental practice, which operated with second shift hours. When she had become a dentist, she had definitely wanted to be available during the evenings. She believed that people should not have to take time off from work or school to see a dentist. Bonnie was always available around their schedules. She wanted them to come to her office a lot so that she could help them.

Her friends from dental school were not really her friends. She had only talked to the other students now and then. She had really wanted to go to medical school. But medical schools were not desperate for students. So dental school was good because she wanted to stop the senseless belief dentures were inevitable.

And she had to keep up with her trucking company. She had gotten her commercial driver license when she had taken over her uncle's trucking company. Uncle Louie had left her the business when he had died, so that she could to medical school. They both thought that cancer treatment was being handled by poets instead of problem solving researchers. Bonnie liked to use chelation therapy and resurfacing treatments, like lasers. Sand off or grind off, the bad part, then wait for the new part to grow. Or eat something that would bond to the bad part, chelate, and carry it away.

She wanted to work in medical research. But the waiting lists for medical schools were long. And the drug dealing traffic with the mafia takeover in Kentucky had cut into her trucking company's profits. So Bonnie finished dental school when Carl Silas had co-signed a private loan that she used for college. And she would go to medical school when the very first medical school accepted her.

She consoled herself with things, such as that she used her Lotus Trucking Company to ship recyclable materials with the railways. That was something that she had started. Bonnie liked conservation, renewable resources, and solar power. She wanted to be part of a solution. Her grandfather had worked for the Paducah railways. Bonnie did not think that the truckers and railways competed for loads. She thought that they should work together with shipments. Bonnie wanted to protect both industries. The railways could carry more larger items than a single truck.

So because not all recyclable materials could be handled everywhere, the railways would collect and transport the remaining recyclable materials that needed to be handled at the other processing plants in different cities. Bonnie was helping shape a better future for her children.

And she could run most of the trucking company from her office at home. With Carl Silas teaching evening classes at the medical school, she was not challenged by her need to please him, and her need to offer dental appointments at night. She had websites for both of her businesses so that she could give people access to any new information that she would find. Bonnie wanted the best. And she always wanted it fast. Like today. Now.

The trucking company was very important to her. She liked the business, the loads, and the people that she would meet. But when they had first married, her meager trucking company salary had been very small, as compared to what Carl Silas earned as a physician at the medical school. With him, she could now live in a large house without burglaries. She could be part of a social solution to world issues with her elevated status and social contacts. But Bonnie was doing more of the physical work, than office paperwork, by killing the dope dealers with that problem. The judicial system would not prosecute the dope dealers when there was drug payoff money. She had no choice with her murders, none at all.

In south Louisville, Kentucky, the first home that she had owned, had been burglarized each day, after the drug gangs had taken over the city. The thieves put filth and anything else, in her food in the refrigerator. They had also, put something vile in the biotin shampoo that she always bought from the health food store. Her glistening, blonde hair was almost dissolved by that contaminated shampoo. When she had came home, and found the grass clippings tossed all over the comforter on her bed, she knew that somebody had been breaking in her home. She had cut the grass the day before. Then the grass clippings were left on her bed.

And she knew that those dope gang members paid about a buck a week to have other people commit murders and burglaries for them. They were nothing but slime that walked and talked. Dope dealers only resembled people. They were like the people that had fed Christians to lions, or had nailed Jesus Christ to a cross. Feeding people to lions and placing nails in human flesh, were sadistic, barbaric behaviors that only satisfied a need to inflict pain. The burglars had put those grass clippings on her bed to show her how they had hurt her. There should be a way to DNA test for that kind of disgusting, deviant human development, like any birth defect. She thought that dope gang members were vomit in clothing.

She was shocked to discover that thieves were making her sick. Bonnie had been ill because of the thieves that had broken into her home. Her life was torn apart by the constant expense of repairs, because the thieves had simply broken her things. Vandalism and burglaries had turned her into a penniless insomniac with nightmares. Those things that had happened to her had made Carl Silas an even more pleasant, desirable choice.

Bonnie had been shocked when he had asked her to marry him. She had went to see him for a medical office appointment about the tapeworms. There had not been any laboratory test results that had showed the presence of anymore of the parasite. Bonnie had been free of the hookworms. He had given her a prescription for an antibiotic, amoxicillin, to help her with any infection that may be left. And then he had said that he wanted to marry her. She had looked at him, said okay, and then had just left the office with her written prescription.

Being used to dealing with men, she mostly just agreed. And then, she had went to the first floor of the hospital and had gotten the prescription filled. Carl Silas had walked into the pharmacy and had said that he was talking about marrying her that day. Bonnie had told him okay, again, and had thanked him for the prescription. She had told him that she had to leave quickly for an appointment.

That was how she handled weird behavior. Bonnie went on with her business. She did what needed to get done. She had just thought that Carl Silas was having a strange day and that she should not make the situation worse by involving herself.

She had thought that he would later, probably just say something like, "Could you not see that things were just a little different for me that day. And that maybe you should have side stepped the issue until my coffee, or the doughnuts had kicked in with the sugar and the caffeine, to help a tired, frazzled person, like me that day, get back into the game." She would just go on being content with the fact that people would regroup, collect themselves, and would strike out again after a break.

That had happened on a Friday. Bonnie always had her phone turned off, but would usually listen to the messages as they were left on the answering machine. She read her emails when they arrived. Lotus Trucking needed to compete with more grace. She wanted her drivers catered to by her, and pampered. Bonnie's interests in recycling and solar power were important to her as a way for her trucks to turn a greater profit. Heating the tractors without using any fuel was good for the drivers and for Lotus. Carl Silas had telephoned on both Saturday and Sunday to leave messages. He had said, that he was serious and that she had said okay.

She thought about how she had transferred to three different universities after the mafia takeover of Kentucky. When she went to the University of Kentucky, she had transferred in with too many credit hours. Her engineering courses were from a different college. The gangs at the University of Louisville had vandalized her car each and every day. She just stopped going to class. Bonnie could have taken the city bus. But she needed to have her car available for her job in Louisville. So, at U of K, after attending for just a few semesters, she was no longer eligible for the federal student loans. After that long drive to Lexington, so that she could get a college degree, and to stop the Louisville thieves from damaging her car, she was now not going to have enough money for her college tuition.

Part 668 of CFR 34, about the student loans, stipulated that if a student attempted to earn a degree that required 120 credit hours, then that student could only receive the federal loans while taking no more than a total of 180 credit hours. That federal regulation had made a horrible problem for Bonnie. The 150% regulation did not consider the fact that maybe only thirty of her transferred credit hours would apply to her new degree, when she had transferred into U of K with a total of 150 credit hours. People that were forced to move due to a job layoff might only be able to borrow enough federal loan money for one college class, before they were denied financial aid, even if they had never borrowed a federal student loan before. U of K had an appeal process to bypass the 150% regulation for special consideration. But the appeals were denied because U of K was not very interested in graduates. The university had a near 50% drop out rate.

Bonnie had tried to have CFR 34 changed by contacting the United States Senate, Congress, and the Office of the U.S. President. Bonnie had paid cash for all her transferred college courses, before going to U of K. She had too many credit hours that would not be used for her degree. And nobody could take away what she had learned in those extra courses. But she still did not have any more money for college. And she could not borrow any more. Now a possible husband, Carl Silas Blake, had appeared in her life. Marrying Carl Silas would give her a co-signer for some loan money with collateral.

Sunday night, she listened again to the messages that he had left. He had also left his home phone number. She had tried to determine why she did not want to marry this man. Bonnie always said okay to things because she could always work those things out later. And Carl Silas Blake, M.D., he was serious. She could win with this move. A physician for a husband would be a good push for her future at a medical school. She was very interested in using lasers for cancer treatment. And she really was not doing anything else right now to keep her from marrying him. She liked to talk to him. But she could also talk to just about anybody about anything. He was attractive, intelligent, and not shy. She liked all of those things.

Even if she said okay now, she could say, not okay, later. So she had telephoned him and left a message. She had just said, "This is Bonnie. Yes, Okay." Then she had started a six hour soak in a hot bubble bath while watching cable television on Sunday night. At eleven o'clock that night, her doorbell rang. She answered the door with dripping wet hair while she was wearing her torn, fifteen year old bathrobe. Carl Silas was standing there on her front porch. That is when she started doing everything his way.

Bonnie just looked at him and said, "Now what?" Carl Silas said that he thought that he should come over since she had waited two days to call him.

She said, "Look, I am soaking wet. I was in a bubble bath and watching a cheap love story on television. I did not check my phone messages until tonight. So do you want to come in and talk, or just leave messages, again?" Carl Silas walked in her front door as if he had walked in her front door all of the time. He was assertive. And she liked that, too.

As he entered her home, she decided to be nice and easy going. Bonnie was more than apt to throw him out if she decided not to listen. But she had already made up her mind. That was a deal that she was going to close. She had wanted it. She had wanted the marriage with the security.

And he was not even ugly, which did not really matter to her. Chocolate candy bars were pretty, too. And when you chewed them, they would taste the same, but not look so pretty anymore. But an unattractive husband could give her unattractive children, no matter which way she would comb their hair. Yes, she was going to do this. And she was glad that he was attractive.

Bonnie had fixed some hot tea while they were talking. Carl Silas had said that he would try her hot tea. She had told him that she took him seriously, and wanted to know what he was looking for and expecting. She had acted like she was negotiating a contract in which she was only trying to offer a service. The deal was wanted by her, and she was going to please her client by meeting his needs.

He had said that he did not want to be alone, that he wanted a relationship. And he talked about his interests in medicine. She had noticed by the way that he was talking, that he thought being a physician was about being important. Bonnie had always thought that being a physician was about solving problems for other people and about opening a door for her into research. She had worked lots of days without any sleep, many times, in the past. She liked to stay busy and to accomplish things.

She was a person that liked to labor, to learn, and to search in her life. Bonnie believed that physical and mental activities used a different part of her brain. She had worked several jobs that made her lift and sort out orders for customers. And just the same as painting or fixing her plumbing at home, she would notice a change in her functioning. So she would try to include reading, as much as possible, into her daily activities.

She had just told him that day, "I do not find you repulsive, like your intelligence, and like the way that you stay physically fit. And okay, I believe that I could have a relationship with you. But I am busy and do not want to play around."

Bonnie had looked at him directly and intensely. Then she said, as she would always say later, "What do you think?" She wanted him to be happy like all her clients.

Carl Silas said that they should do it, get married. So they had medical tests for any diseases, because she was not stupid, just wanted safety, and was careful. Then when the medical tests results were back, they got married. They did not have a ceremony planned. There was not a party. Both of them went to work, to their jobs without taking any time off. And she did not want any wedding gifts. Bonnie did not have any relatives to tell because she never spoke to them.

The lack of gifts was surprising to Carl Silas. But Bonnie just said, "We do not have to write thank you notes. Besides, I do not like

Christmas gifts, either. I am too choosy about everything. I like what I like. And that is only what I buy."

But she did offer a spectacular feast when a few of his friends came over to his house to celebrate. Bonnie would always have refreshments available in their home. In just a few days after she had met Carl Silas, she had married him. Bonnie took over his house like a project. She ask him what he liked and did not like about the house. Then she changed the house to please him.

And he knew that she was research oriented before they were married. Bonnie liked to learn about everything. Like any athlete, she would push herself for an extra strain. He was so much less demanding with himself. She lulled him into a happy spot in his life. And then she spoiled him, catered to him, and gave him everything that he wanted.

She never went to sleep with him when they were first married. She would wait until he went to sleep, then slip out of the bed. Bonnie really did not know enough about him so that she could relax and go to sleep. She just wanted the marriage. But after a few weeks, she was more comfortable with him, and able to go to sleep much easier.

Still, she would occasionally go to the guest bedroom to read late at night after he went to sleep. Sometimes she would fall asleep with the book in her hand. Once she woke up in the dark, and looked at the blue clock display. She knew that she was in the guest bedroom because of the clock. Carl Silas was in the bed beside her. He had found her and turned off the light. His arm was wrapped around her.

Her tapeworm dilemma and constant thieves had given her insomnia. But those situations were better. Still another time, she woke up at about two o'clock in the morning, and went to watch television downstairs. After about two hours of watching the comedy shows, she must have fallen asleep. When she woke up, Carl Silas was snuggled up against her on the sofa. He was asleep and had not turned off the lights or the television. She wondered if he would find her if she went to sleep in a closet with the door closed. He was comfortable to her. And she had made sure that she was extremely comfortable to him.

Carl Silas was a doctor that Bonnie could recommend. And she did not like most physicians. The dope trade had created a medical industry of abusive people. Her old friend, Jan Wilks, had her leg amputated by one of those butchers, Thomas Lube, M.D. He was an orthopedic surgeon that made his money performing surgeries instead of treating illnesses. His surgical fee was larger than his fee for treatment. So Lube would simply amputate a limb that would never grow back and collect a lot of money for the operation.

Now Jan was in a wheelchair, a motorized scooter, because Lube had told her that he had to amputate the lower part of her leg that was swelling. Bonnie had been working out of town when Jan had the surgery. She could have told Jan that the swelling could be controlled by elevating her leg, and with hot and cold treatments to move the fluid in her legs. Jan had never elevated her leg and was smoking.

Bonnie had only talked to her one time about what she knew about sports injuries and swelling. Then she had let the subject drop out of the way. The leg was gone without any good reason. Jan had banged her leg in an automobile accident. The surgeon was a viper that worked in a city that was controlled by the mafia.

And now Bonnie knew, but never mentioned, that Jan was using drugs to keep her mind blank. Bonnie had only went to see her once. She talked with Jan, gave her a stack of books from the bookstore with a book bag, and an inflatable bathtub for soaking her legs. Bonnie hated drugs, drug users, and drug dealers. And she knew that Jan was using drugs so that she could escape the pain of knowing that Lube had just wanted to make her a cripple.

That was different from her other friends that she would see or run into. When she was buying cheese for a snack, at a Save Now Grocery off of Tenth Street, in Jeffersonville, Indiana, Bonnie saw Cheryl Thompson walk in with a small boy. Cheryl spotted Bonnie. She heard Cheryl tell the boy that the woman over there was Bonnie.

The small boy ran to Bonnie and hugged her legs. Then Bonnie felt his wet tears on her summer tanned knees. He said that Bobby did not come home and that the police said that he may have been a runaway. Bonnie picked him up and hugged him close. He cried into her shirt. Runaway, would be a way for Hanson, Cheryl's husband, to explain why his son had left while not facing the facts of the drug world.

Hanson would say his son was wild, not appreciative, and left in a spoiled temper. Hanson believed that he was always correct, did his best, and closed his eyes to the rest of the world. He would let somebody else take care of pollution control. Hanson was always tired from his job and only wanted to go home.

Bonnie did not believe that Bobby was a runaway. He was probably a victim of gang violence. And Bobby most likely still thought that girls were only stupid. Hanson most certainly still did to this day. With that kind of a father, a hard worker that did not get involved with issues, Bobby may have problems coming home to ask for help.

Bonnie used to babysit for Bobby when she had worked with Cheryl at Simby Restaurant. Bobby was about four years old then, and would be over sixteen years old now. Maybe nobody had told Bobby not to say that he did not want to be a pick. Bonnie already assumed that Bobby was missing due to an attack by the drug gangs.

Then Cheryl walked over. She told Bonnie that Bobby had always talked about Bonnie with little Henry. Bobby had told Henry that girls were stupid and that he did not like them. That would have echoed Hanson's words, that girls were stupid.

Bonnie was never paid for babysitting with Bobby. She would just go over to their house when they had asked, if she had the free time. Then she would usually babysit, cook a meal, wash dishes, do some laundry, and clean the house a little.

When Bobby had explained that he thought that girls were stupid, Bonnie had told him that he had a right to have his own ideas and opinions. They would usually munch down on her favorite of fried chicken with French fries, and watch a movie. So she would stop at the grocery, buy the chicken, and some cottage cheese for a salad. She never knew what Cheryl might have in the refrigerator.

And she would not have eaten any food out of the refrigerator anyway.

She had told Bobby about brushing his teeth and cleaning his mouth, so that his teeth would last a lifetime. Bonnie always carried a toothbrush. And they would both brush their teeth. Then they would drink glasses of water while they watched the movie. Bonnie told Bobby to swish the water around in his mouth for a few minutes before he swallowed. She had let him know that those little pieces of food would rot in his mouth.

And she had tried to include exercise. But Bobby did not like to walk around the block. They would start walking. Then Bonnie would have to carry Bobby because his little legs would teeter out of energy. He would always contend that girls were dumb, even while she carried him. She would ask if she could jog while she carried him. He was okay with that for a short time. Then he would say that he might vomit. So they would mostly eat healthy snacks, work on personal hygiene, try doing push ups with other exercises, and watch movies.

Bobby's mom, Cheryl said, "Bonnie, we do not know what to do without Bobby being found. Hanson does not sleep much. We just worry. And Henry cries."

"Cheryl, you know that they put in the dope gangs. Anything can happen with gangs," Bonnie told her bluntly.

"Hanson says that he pays his taxes and owns his home. He does not get involved with other things. The police are doing absolutely nothing. And we know it," Cheryl spoke back in a whisper.

Bonnie had to go. She just said, "I am sorry. I will do what I can. If I learn of anything to help, I will phone you. I do need to go. I will always remember your hug, Henry. We will find Bobby." Then she left the store.

Hanson had done nothing to stop the terror. And they had taken his son. There was not much you could to make people motivated. They paid their taxes, like Hanson, and expected to have a country to live in. The problem was that the government was corrupt. They took your tax dollars. And you had to protect yourself.

That was nearly the way that Bonnie had talked to her husband, Carl Silas. She would come home, and he would say that he wanted to explain. She was always tired.

Bonnie would just say, "Carl Silas, I just want to take a shower and go to sleep. If you want to tell me your stories, which are lies, just write them down. I can read them when I wake up. And remember, I like to recycle. So just use the memo board by the phone, so that I can wipe away the message. Live your life the way that you want to, Carl Silas. I do not want your lies because I do not care. I trust you to have privacy. When I want to leave, I will pack up and go. I am not leaving. I am not packing. I do not need to know all your details. Be your own person. I just want to go to sleep. And you know that I do trust you. Now what do you want to do? I am tired. So I will stand here and look at you, until you tell me. Because I do like to look at you."

He would smile, kiss her, and walk away with an appreciative, "Sleep well," tossed back at her.

That way she could avoid his opinions. Carl Silas liked Carl Silas. He was smooth and self-centered. Bonnie was a caregiver, a helping person that was born with too much trust for others. She had married Carl Silas Blake for safety. Giving him his own personal space would keep him safe with his own needs fulfilled. He thought that she trusted him. But really, Bonnie just did not want to be bothered with the details.

He was extremely attractive and intelligent. So Bonnie made the best of her situation. But when he talked, she sort of heard his voice like the buzzing of bees. After the beginning of their marriage, when she had found out that her husband was so intensely self-centered, she had simply let him always have his way. She never argued. Never trying to control him, Bonnie could use her energy for the interests in her life. For her, Carl Silas was like doing a push up, or curling another set of ten, at the gym. She had gained one more thing. He allowed her to check off, married, on her list of things to do.

Every person had the right to live their life in the ways that they wanted. But if Carl Silas ever was to become involved with any other woman, then Bonnie would leave him. She had her own secrets, too. One of them was, that he would not respond too well if he was told that she only wanted and needed him. She was never going to love him. She was just taking what she could get in life. Right now, Bonnie Blake was doing the best that she could.

Carl Silas was a physician. She liked the money. And she always believed that she was her own person. If he was sick or injured, she would care for him. But they did not need to agree on everything.

Bonnie had her part in the war against the mafia. And Carl Silas had not any part in that war.

After all, Bonnie Blake would kill any pick that she came across. Her muscles would tighten with her hatred when she met one. She would vibrate with disgust when she thought about how the picks tortured and swindled people. Carl Silas was a break from that life. He did not torture her. And she liked his intelligence.

Ignorant people could truly irritate Bonnie. She was a realist. Being self-sufficient, she did not depend on any belief that Carl Silas would care for her if she was injured or ill for a long time. Bonnie would always look like a classy, magazine model because she valued a healthy, attractive appearance.

Her good looks kept Carl Silas interested in having children. Their kids would be extremely attractive. He liked to talk about their children a lot now. She was young. And that would give them the later years in their lives to be alone because their kids would be grown by then. He liked to bring his friend's kids over to talk to Bonnie when they would meet people at a store.

"Okay, Carl Silas. If you want a child, then you shall have a child. A child to look like his father. Now can we find the yogurt and cheese for my salad? Kids needs lots of calcium," she once told him in the grocery.

Bonnie thought about how having a child would curtail her war activities. Her breakneck jogs would be slower. She might get caught in a murder. They would give the child to Carl Silas after the baby had slowed her down enough to bring her to an unpleasant end. But like all warriors, Bonnie never thought about being caught or about imprisonment, because she would die in battle.

She did want to have the war and her own kids, too. And Carl Silas, he would keep finding ways to bring kids to their home. He liked Greg's little boy, Christian. Greg was another one of the physicians that worked at the hospital with Carl Silas. Bonnie was not surprised when he told her that he wanted Christian to spend Saturday night with them, while Martha and Greg went to Nashville, Tennessee to see a show.

Christian was only four years old and afraid to be alone with strangers. But he was happy enough when Bonnie showed him that she had made his favorite dinner, lasagna, with his favorite snacks, fudge brownies and popcorn balls. Carl Silas had action, adventure television planned for the evening. Arnold Schwarzenegger, Bruce Lee, and Jean-Claude Van Damme were fun for Christian to watch in the movies. Bonnie was pumped up by all the fight scenes in the movies.

At about eleven o'clock that night, little Chris was fading to sleep very fast. Carl Silas said that she should put him in a bed. Chris was away from his parents. And he was supposed to be having his night of entertainment, too. Going to bed was not fun for children. Bonnie wondered how Carl Silas had spent his childhood. She did not really care. She just wondered.

Christian hugged her tighter as he was leaning across her lap. Bonnie said automatically, "No." She had never said the word, no, to her husband before. And as soon as she had said it, she remembered that she never refused him because she always gave him his way. Kids would get her into trouble. She could already feel the problem coming her way.

Then Carl Silas just looked at her, and said, "Alright. I will carry Christian to bed."

Bonnie said, "No," again.

Carl Silas replied, even stronger, "What I said was that Christian is falling asleep and needs to go to bed."

Bonnie just said, "No, he can stay up." She was really inspired by the movies and felt like Carl Silas was a major wimp. But she was not going to fight.

Then Carl Silas looked at Christian, and said, "People sleep in beds, not on the sofa."

Christian looked at Carl Silas, and said, "My dad takes a nap on the couch."

Christian hugged her even tighter. So Bonnie asked, "Christian, do you want to go to bed or to stay up?"

Christian said quietly, "Stay up."

"Okay. Then you can stay up," Bonnie announced.

Carl Silas delivered his decision by saying, "Little boys will sleep in beds. I am responsible for that child tonight. I am the one that works with his father. I said that he will go to bed."

Bonnie never disagreed with him. He thought that maybe she was ill or just tired. She had always trusted his judgment. Bonnie relied on him.

Bonnie said, once more, "No. And do not say that, again. Christian is pinching me so hard that he will draw blood."

Carl Silas reached for Christian, as he told the little boy, "Christian, do not hurt Bonnie."

Bonnie looked at Carl Silas quickly, and ordered, "Carl Silas, do not touch Christian. He has me in his little fingers hold. Those little pinchers can hurt."

Carl Silas and Bonnie were going to fight. She felt a tear start in her eye. Bonnie had done everything to avoid any sort of fight with Carl Silas throughout their entire marriage. She wanted to be safe and warm. Her insomnia was becoming less of a problem as she relaxed more, and more, after the years that she had spent with the Louisville drug dealers that had been burglarizing her home.

Bonnie said, "He can stay up."

Then she asked, because she wanted to know, "Christian, this is only a question. You can stay up. But I am curious and want to know, if you would go to bed in a strange room, so that I would not have to fight with and leave my husband? Or would you stay up in the television room with us?"

"Stay up," Christian told her.

Those tears in her eyes were obvious to Carl Silas. So he just watched her. He had never seen her cry. He had never heard her talk about leaving him. He thought that she must feel ill. And that he should care for her. He was trying to get kids, his kids into his home.

Then Bonnie asked Christian, "Would you help me for a few moments? I want Carl Silas to hold you. And I am going to hold your hand so that you will know that he is not going to take you to the bedroom."

Bonnie placed Christian on her husband's lap. And she held his little hand. She thought about how she had pampered and spoiled little Bobby when she had been his babysitter. The drug gangs, and she had just known that, had killed Bobby in that organized crime network that Louisville had become. She had phoned Cheryl that morning. Cheryl had told her that Bobby had been found, beaten to death, near a dumpster by the Second Street bridge.

She thought about Bobby as she curled under her husband's arm and as she wiped the tears from her eyes on her T-shirt sleeve. She hugged his arm and held the little boy's hand. Carl Silas felt her cry harder. His off night had changed course into a sad ordeal with his wife crying.

He did not know how long the crying would last. And he did not know what to do about it. He did not like for her to cry in front of children. People might think that he beat her. But he let Christian stay on his lap like she wanted. And Bonnie went to sleep, curled under his arm, with her tiny sniffles.

When Bonnie woke up, Christian was gone. She asked Carl Silas where he had put Christian. Carl Silas answered, "It is two o'clock in the morning. Greg took Christian home at a little after one. Do you think that you will be crying some more tonight? I had no idea how long that was going to last. I wanted us to get used to having kids in our home. You could have scared Christian."

Then Bonnie stretched across his lap with a small pillow. And she asked, in a way to distract him away from her earlier tears, "Are we going to watch more T.V.?"

Carl Silas looked at her, and said, "That is what I am doing. I never watch late night television. This is intense male action. You are always up in the wee hours of the morning."

Bonnie did not start crying again. She had her head on the pillow on his lap. He was watching her, and the movie at the same time, with an expression that he would have reserved for a monster in a movie. This was his off night that he had planned with action movies for Christian. Now he just wanted to watch her like a laboratory experiment. Eventually, she hugged him slightly and snuggled tighter. He thought that she would probably start talking about leaving him again just when he was all inspired with the movies. Somehow, he knew that his good feelings were going to slide away.

So Carl Silas, just said, "I do not want you to cry in front of children. People might think that I abuse you. So the problem is?"

Bonnie snuggled and stretched across his lap. She was still sleepy. And she said, "I have never, in all this time fought with you. I have that little feeling that I am going to go to sleep again. My inomnia never bothered you until you started missing me at night. I believe that my sleepless nights are improving. And Christian did not see me cry."

Carl Silas replied, "No, that is not it. And, yes, your eyes were flooded with tears. I have never seen that before."

Then Bonnie responded, "I need to get something to drink."

He thought that she was trying to avoid the subject and to get away from him. And he was pretty sure that she was sick. So he just pushed her back onto his lap when she tried to get up. He said, "You can sip some of my orange juice."

Bonnie was surprised when he pushed her back down. But she was also still a little weepy and languid. So she just stared at the T.V., and said, "You know that I do not drink after another person. I will get my own drink." She was really thirsty and needed more than just some sips.

He just stared at her as he replied, "My orange juice will not hurt you. I have kissed you more than a hundred times." Then he leaned down and kissed her again, as he said, "Hundred and one times."

She started to get up again. He just knew that she was sick and needed to rest. He thought that maybe, she would fall down after all that crying. This time, Carl Silas, crossed his leg over her to hold her on the sofa.

The thought raced through her mind that he was a lot of work. She used her hand and fingers to massage the ball of his foot. She touched the tender spot on his foot. And he jerked his leg. Then she pushed his leg away and jumped up off the couch. Carl Silas grabbed for her. Bonnie moved her arm away from him. That was a shock. She had never jerked away from him before. But she wanted to get some grapefruit juice in the kitchen without a fight. A fight would keep her thirsty for a longer time.

She got a solemn look on her face and said, "I am sorry for jerking away from you. I know that you will not hurt me."

Then she hurried toward the kitchen as she said, "And if I do burst into tears, I will step into the closet and wrap the sleeves of the sweaters and coats around me." Her temper was sparking. But she never lost control.

He walked after her to the kitchen. His temper was rising, too, because he wanted to straighten out the problem and get on with his off night of fun. He stepped near the sink, next to her, and said, "I do not want you to be afraid of disagreeing with me. I want you to fight with me. And I did want Christian to go to bed when he was falling asleep. Now why were you crying? I have never seen you cry before, in all this time."

Bonnie placed her elbows on the kitchen table as she leaned her head down to put her chin in her hands. Her temper was flying high. But she did not want to fight. She stared at Carl Silas in a slow, speculative fashion.

Then she said, "You have not been around children very much. Children always cry when they have to go to bed. Christian was alone without his parents tonight. His time should have been happy. And I wanted you to be a male role model that he would like. Kids just fall asleep when and where they want to, if I am the person doing the babysitting. I really did not want you to be the babysitter monster."

Now Carl Silas was leaning against the refrigerator door. She wanted the grapefruit juice that was on the top shelf. Bonnie just stared at him while she was trying to remember what he had said. A long time ago, she had conveniently stopped listening to what he said. Now what he said was obviously going to be involved in what happened. And she needed to listen to him as if there was going to be an exam about the conversation.

Carl Silas was angry now. She had always given him his way without any challenge. And he appeared to be wrong in this instance, because he really did not want Christian to cry. So he crossed his arms across his chest, and asked, "Why did you cry?" He did not add, I want to know why you talked about leaving me. He was trying to get some kids into his house.

The word cry sounded like an accusation to her. She had shown weakness. Bonnie squinted her eyes as she said, "I really want the grapefruit juice. I am trying to remember why I cried?"

Carl Silas stretched his six foot six inch frame casually across the front of the refrigerator. He looked doubtful, as he said, "Trying to remember why you were crying. I thought that your whole world had collapsed. I wondered if I needed to find a stopwatch so that

I could time the event. Could have been a world record. And, you talked about leaving me. I thought that we had agreed to start having kids, now."

Bonnie had it now. World collapsed. She would use that. So she said, "Yes, that was it. I had never thought about leaving you before. I would leave if I had to go. But I would not enjoy it. I would do it. And spend a lot of time trying to find a new husband. And with all that work for me to do, little Christian, was still not going to go to bed so that he could help me. I had to fight you, instead. There were only a few tears. And yes, we can start having kids now." Bonnie walked to the kitchen cabinets.

She spoke slowly to him, "You married a woman. You seemed to like those. In this culture, men are not supposed to cry. And yes, I have never cried in front of you. When I was very young, I stopped crying. My older brother used to harass me so that I would cry. I just stopped crying. Many mornings, before I left for elementary school, I would have fights with my parents. And believe me when I say that I will not tolerate a negative word about my parents. But they were trying to shape me into their kind of lifestyle. Still I never cried during those fights. And I would never fit into their kind of life. I am adventure born. I can cry or not cry. I was probably just feeling relaxed tonight, in our own home. So I will try to act tougher and not cry. But I am not going to grow a moustache."

He looked at her like he was trying to make up his mind about something. She was wearing his yellow T-shirt. Most of his clothes had been given to her as he had bought new ones. His jackets and shirts were fine for her, even if he was over seven inches taller.

She would just roll up the sleeves. But his trousers and jeans were really much too big for her.

Then he said, "You would probably get a rash if you had a moustache. You would not wash it enough. Most people do not wash their moustaches enough. A moustache can hold bacteria."

"I do not want a moustache, anyway. I only wear your T-shirts and clothes when you give them to me. I am not trying to dress like a man. But you never wear skirts and dresses, so I do have to buy those," she told them.

He watched her back down from the fight. As he took a beer out of the refrigerator, he said, "Only drink about twenty-five percent grapefruit juice to water. Reduce your sugar. You were crying." He was still pushing for a fight. He had never even noticed that they did not argue.

Bonnie said, as she watched him grabbed another bottle of beer, "Okay. Crying. Guilty. Would like a pizza and some veggies with dip while I am in here? I was going to put one in the oven."

Carl Silas said, "Fine." He thought that he would just let it go.

So Bonnie, continued, "And how many slices of pizza would you prescribe?" Even though she was almost asleep and would not be eating, she gave him complete control.

Carl Silas prescribed, "Two slices of pizza after crying." He watched her pour out the grapefruit juice and water according to his orders.

The crying had scared him. Bonnie drank the entire glass full of grapefruit and water.

"And like I said, I can cry or not cry. I want the grapefruit juice," she told him as she poured a glass full of only grapefruit juice. Then she drank all of that.

"So you get beer. And I drink water. Because now, water is only what I want for my teeth," Bonnie added.

Carl Silas only said as he walked back to the television room with his beers, "I was not the one that was crying. Beer might depress you. The diluted juice was only a suggestion. I am trying to get my kids into my house."

She took the pizza out of the oven and sliced it. Then she carried the pizza, veggies, and her fresh glass of water to the television room. Carl Silas was drinking his second beer. She curled up next to him on the sofa. Bonnie was always cold and snuggling close for his warmth. He kept leaning over to look at her.

He finally said, "Are you going to cry if your pizza is cold?" He waited for her to reply to his remark. Then he asked, "Bonnie are you going to eat the pizza?"

But Bonnie was already asleep and dreaming about Jean-Claude Van Damme. Her husband's action adventure night with Arnold Schwarzenegger and Jean-Claude Van Damme was good for her, too. She like to watch the fight scenes that were so much related to the other part of her life, her fight against dope.

She woke up at about five o'clock in the morning. Carl Silas had drank four beers. He was stroking her hair. Then he asked, "Are you going to eat some pizza?" She ask him if he wanted her to eat. Because he wanted her to, she ate one slice of pizza to please him. When she had been single, she never had to put on a charade about pleasing anyone. But to keep him happy, she just snuggled close to him.

Then he said, "You talked about leaving me. I do not want you to leave me. We are supposed to have kids. I know that everyday is not going to be a party. And I have noticed how you keep our lives positioned with happiness. When you cried, that was probably the first sadness that I saw in you, since we got married, except for your medical school longing." He moved the pillow, that was under her head, just a little closer to her face.

"Your hair is so soft. I tried to get the tangles out with my fingers so that it would all be smooth. Did I wake you? Have you ever cried when you brushed the tangles from your hair? If I had a brush right now, I would brush the tangles out of your long, blonde hair. Your silky hair is something that I have always liked. You always stay in shape and look great," he told her.

So she asked, "Now are you going to put me under a microscope so that you can find out what makes me cry? I said that I did not want to leave you. That for sure, would make me cry with all that hard work in finding a new husband. And I will not cry in front of you again, if you become so uncomfortable. No law says that you have to hold me. I just like it when you do snuggle with me."

"Sounds good to have peace again. I did not win you in a contest. But I am happy that you married me so quickly without a chase. I appreciate all that you do, even if I did not spend a lot of time trying to bring you home with me. Did you like having Christian here?" he asked.

Bonnie cuddled closer and said, "Yes, I like kids. Christian included. And we will have kids. Our kids will have rules. And everything was going great until you almost made him cry. Just because he is a boy does not mean that he will not cry, not be hurt by your orders. He held me so tight when he was afraid of going to bed in a strange room. Those bedrooms are strange to him. Why could you not just let him doze off a little in my arms? All kids do that. I like to help you, and to help other people, too. Christian was pleading with his whole tiny person. I wanted to have fun. But anyway, for tomorrow, do you know what you want me to cook?"

He told her that maybe he would just cook something when he got up tomorrow. Probably cook pigs-in-the-blankets. His famous biscuits wrapped around hotdogs, baked to a golden perfection that he liked with Chinese hot mustard and duck sauce. Then maybe, he thought, she would not think about him as the babysitter monster.

Bonnie told him strongly, "I can cook. Crying is not like being crippled in a wheelchair. You think that I showed weakness and vulnerability. Like I said, if the crying bothered you, then I will not cry again." She did not add that he acted like an ogre, that he was selfish, and that she did not love him. Bonnie just mellowed out the tiny conflict with soft caresses. He was her shelter in the storm of life and adversity. Carl Silas would be enough for her until she found something better.

So Carl Silas asked, "Would you cry if I changed the television channel? You did cry pretty hard."

Bonnie answered slowly, languidly, in soft whispered words, "Maybe, only if I was watching Jean-Claude Van Damme, Bruce Lee, or Arnold Schwarzenegger. Please, do drink another beer, Carl Silas. I am asleep." He was a little more abrasive when he was drinking liquor. And he was also more honest, more open with his thoughts and opinions. But she really could not keep him in a drunken stupor all the time, no matter how much easier his moods were to please when he was drinking beers. She did not have to put forth that extra little, are you happy kind of conversation, when he drank beers, because she did not have to talk at all then.

He was not going to let it go. He only replied arrogantly, "Would you cry if I was drunk? Like maybe, after four beers? Would you cry if I poured beer in your hair? Cry those big, racking sobs like I heard?"

"No, I do not care what you do. Never have. Beer is good for my hair. So drink another beer. I have a very renowned doctor's orders for water, less sugar. From you. And only you. I am a crier, guilty of being a woman. And I do like being a woman, Carl Silas, because I really do like to be held by men like you, an awful lot," Bonnie bounced back.

He thought that she would not like for him to keep drinking his beers. But she only bought them so that he would drink. That was just another sign that he would probably never cross over into the rest of her life. He guessed wrong a lot. She would keep him out of her war, always and forever. And she would never feel guilty about any of it. She hated and killed all drug dealers.

The next day, Bonnie sliced her pigs-in-the-blankets and put them over a cottage cheese and lettuce salad. Carl Silas ate two with barbecue sauce. Then he sliced four of the biscuit wrapped hotdogs over a lettuce and tomato salad. Dinner was cooked by him. Crying must have been very frightening for Carl Silas.

Chapter 3   Battle On

Bonnie thought about how Carl Silas was spending a lot more time with her in conversation. They were talking more and more. That was too much talking for Bonnie. He was trying to keep a handle of control on his marriage. And Bonnie wanted him to change back to his usually spoiled, selfish attitude. She needed more time alone and less talking. Her approach had always been to give him everything that he wanted, so that he would be happy while she actually did what she wanted, without any questions. Her husband floated around in a fog with the impression that they were in love now and probably would be always together.

Carl Silas did not even know about the extreme amount of gas that Bonnie bought. She did not want him to ask her questions because he would probably remember her answers. Then she would have to keep up on whichever story that she had been telling him. The whole thing would be easier for her if she did not create an alibi. Then she would not have to remember anything about what she had told him. She took a few moments away from that quandary to lull in a hot bubble bath. Eventually, she knew that he would stop fretting over their relationship and relax again.

While Bonnie was soaking in the soft, billowy, fern scented bubbles, she thought about how she had always dreamed about killing Bert Night. She was always chasing him in her dreams at night, with blood lust pulsing through her veins. She had to grab him, to kill him, to make him gone from this life. Night had terrorized and murdered many people with his cocaine, heroin operation. Her dreams were a constant struggle to get rid of him. She would wake up tired and exhausted from her attempts to snare him. Maybe those dreams would stop when he was dead, when one of her many killing jobs was over and done, when she had that one less fear in her life because Bert Night was gone.

At the times during her wide awake hours, when she thought about how she would kill Bert Night, she would always imagine herself to be in a parking garage. She would happen to come across him in the garage. Bonnie would get that gleam in her eye when she was near her torturer. She would say his name, Bert Night, with cold and vibrant tones. He would come closer to her. As he approached, she would see a broom left in the parking garage by a worker. She would grab the broom from behind her back, out of his sight. As he got closer, Bonnie would stare icily toward him. When he was almost next to her, she would raise the broom and savagely hit his face.

Then he would stumble backward. He would look at her with his shocked, self-centered, all-important stare, and say, "I am Bert Night, the Police Chief."

She would look at his soon-to-be-dead eyes, and say with disgust, "I know who you are, slime."

And the recognition of her threat by this vile, contemptible drug dealer, would appear in his eyes, as he reached for his gun. Bonnie would knock the gun from his hand with the broom and slam the broom into his knee. Bert Night would fall down, as she watched for the fear in his eyes. She would spit the words in his face, "Crawl for your life filth." He would spring up and limp to run away.

Bonnie wanted the chase so his terror would mount. She wanted him to run blindly with insane fright until he would just keep vomiting uncontrollably. She wanted to watch his feeble attempts to save himself, as she sprinted after him. She would run closer, as Bert Night would stumble forward.

"You can not just kill me. I am the chief. Stop this," he would yell back at her.

"No. That is really not what I want. I do not want to stop this. You stop running. I will show you what I can do to drug slime. I want to watch the fear in your eyes. Slow down, now," she would bluntly say.

"Me slow down? You get away from me," he would shout.

"But I only want to get closer. Ever so close."

"I do not want you close. I am the police chief. I told you."

"I heard you. I want to hear you closer."

"You can not do this to me."

"I already am. I am not going to stop. I like this."

He was a drug dealer, and drug dealers were all vicious cowards that would prey on the defenseless, the unsuspecting. There were not any rules of decency involved when you killed a drug dealer. She thought that drug dealers were just supposed to be dead.

Then for the final attack, she would menacingly breathe the words, "Where will you slither? How will you crawl? When you are already dead." And she would raise the broom a few more times as she would mercilessly pound him to death. Bonnie would watch with satisfaction when the blood dripped from his face. That dope dealer would be finally gone according to the fate of any evil menace. He would be killed in pain.

Bonnie enjoyed those dreams and the thoughts of killing that police chief. Bert Night had ruined so many lives with his dope game. Money and power were his mainstays. His group of vagabond thieves had looted her friends. She was concerned about planting new trees, conservation, water purity, and health issues with education. Her people were being put back into prehistoric times with the drug peddler attacks.

She had enjoyed those dreams again last night. They were so vivid. Her muscles probably ached this morning because she must have been fighting pretty hard. She did clench her fists a lot, even when she was wide awake. In her dreams, she was a violent fighting machine that could almost push over buildings with one tiny press of her fingers. That would make her blood race with pleasure. And this morning she was excited and inspired by those dreams.

Today, Bonnie was leaving the Indiana hotel much earlier than her usual five o'clock in the morning. After she had stayed over night, she walked in the darkness to the dumpster and threw away the empty packages from the outlet mall. She liked to shop. And now she needed to go to Columbus, Indiana to pick up a local newspaper. With the accident blocking the expressway, she really had no choice except to spend the night. So she had stayed, instead of driving about one hundred miles around the blocked roads.

Indiana was not the greatest place at this time, but some people in the state were helping to push for the federal charges against Bert Night. When she came out of the gasoline station, in Columbus, she thought that she saw a Black man that looked like Bert Night standing on the parking lot next to her car. Bonnie had been trying to have Bert Night charged for a long time. He walked right up to her. And he called her name, "Bonnie, I am Chief Night. My men talk about you a lot."

"About me?"

"All the time."

"So you know me."

"Yes. I have wanted to meet you," he told her.

Bonnie remembered how she had been killing the men that he had sent to try kill her. Also, she thought about how she was helping to steal the drug payoff bribe money that Night liked to send around.

Bonnie smiled and said, "Chief Night, do you have an office in Columbus, Indiana, now?" She had the feeling that some of his people had tracked her from that Indiana hotel. She wanted Night to be charged by the federal government. If she had to go back to college to earn a law degree just to make that happen, then she would do that.

Chief Night said, "I wanted to talk to you."

Bonnie thought, no, what you want to do is to kill me. That he had been trying to kill her for quite a while, was a very good reason for her to please him now. She told him, "I would be honored. Do you have to be somewhere soon?"

"No, I do not have an appointment this morning. I just came here to check on some things," he replied.

She paused a moment, and then said, "Maybe you should call your office and tell them that you will be seeing someone for about half an hour or so?"

"Nobody knows where I am. I can go back to Louisville anytime that I want," Night said.

Bonnie tensed a moment with that comment. She was not tense with fear, but with pleasure. Knowing that when he would come to kill a person, Night would not tell people where he was going, was a thought that had Bonnie vibrating with the lust for revenge. And she liked that. She knew that they were both going to enjoy an isolated place on this slightly chilly morning.

"I am supposed to meet a friend at a nearby park, just a few minutes away. We are going to jog. I have some baggy sweats in the car and a pair of my husband's track shoes. If you want to come along, I also have an unopened box of fried chicken that I microwaved. My friend will be very impressed with you and all of your accomplishments for Louisville, Kentucky. You could put on a pair of my husband's clean socks and jog. Or, just munch on the chicken and enjoy the park. Just like family. You really should run for some political office. Are you parked close?" Bonnie asked with a fake glow in her eyes.

She only thought about how her friends had been killed for their clothes, their jobs, their homes and then left without any future. Bert Night had ransacked the Caucasian area of south Louisville and created another Black drug slum environment. But Bonnie kept her smile bright and her actions polite. She was solicitous.

Night was staring at her as he said, "My car is in the parking garage. I just walked over to buy a snack."

"You can ride with me. And you are just like my husband. You never wear gloves. Your hands will freeze before my car has warmed up. Put on these gloves. And we can talk in my car," she replied and handed him the gloves. That would keep his fingerprints off of the inside of her car.

Night put on the gloves and followed her to the car. She drove to a secluded area in the park. The sun had not come up yet. So Bonnie looked around intensely for other people in the darkness. There was nobody anywhere near them. But anybody could come to a public park at anytime. Their privacy could be interrupted quickly. The path was a little longer to this part of the park which would help to keep people away. But there was not any door for her to lock in this wide open forest area. She could not make sure that no one saw what was going to happen between her and Night. Bonnie had to watch and listen closely for any other person that might approach.

The dew had settled on the park bench. So she told Night to wait a minute while she put some cardboard on the bench seat. Then she said, "That will not be enough. I will put a blanket over the wet bench. That should keep us dry." Bonnie got the plastic lined stadium blanket from her car and used it to cover the bench. And she got her gym bag from the car.

He was sitting on the bench with his left hand on the bench seat to support himself as leaned forward to pull off his shoes. Night was not even looking at her. He really was a self-absorbed little tyrant. She sat down next to him on the bench. And she felt her muscles flex with a pure rush of power and pleasure. Then Bonnie pulled her camping ax out of her gym bag and chopped off his left hand.

She thought that she had her tent stake hammer with her. But in the darkness, she could only find the travel ax. He had surprised her this morning. Bonnie did not have any time to plan. She did not like to have to run any risks when she killed a dope dealer because there could be too many problems. Even if she was not ecstatic with Carl Silas, she was safe, and warm. And he was intelligent and attractive. She did not need to rush with her murders because she did have a safe home to live in.

So, now she had a big problem with lots of blood on her stadium blanket. That was a mess that was going to take some of her precious time to clean up and could place her in big trouble if she was found in the middle of a sloppy murder. And that was only part of her problem, because Night was still not dead. Bonnie could not even start cleaning up until he was dead. She needed him to be dead really fast so that she could clean up and leave really quick.

Night yelled, "My hand!"

She had hoped that he would not yell while she was trying so hard not to attract attention. But she had already been expecting an outburst when she knew that she was going to have to use the ax and not the hammer. And now she was happy with the ax because she hated Night so much that she liked to hurt him. She just hated the mess with the murder. But she could not keep feeding her pleasure for hurting him, for very long, because of the constant possibility of being caught in the park. Bonnie looked at his severed left hand and said, "What have you done? Did you change your shoes?"

He stared at his left arm without his hand. Bonnie said urgently, "How did you hurt yourself? You need to go to a hospital. I just woke up. We need to take care of this. Where is your hand? How did it fall off? I might have some bandaids. What do you need?"

Then she said again, "Where is your hand? How did you cut yourself? You are bleeding! There is blood everywhere." And she did like to see the blood. She liked to watch his face in pain. But now, he was more aware of the danger and might become suspicious. Those brief seconds of wonder were gone. He reached for his missing hand.

Bonnie said in a promising tone, "They can put your hand back on your wrist. They can re-attach your hand. We need to hurry and save your hand. You might pass out if we wait any longer. Are you going to hurry? You have to hurry." As she said that, she used the ax that she had concealed behind her gym bag to cut into his chest. Bonnie just chopped and chopped. She tried to make Chief Night smaller and smaller. He was a filthy, disgusting drug dealer. Bonnie truly hated and killed all dope dealers.

And she was going to be very tired again. She wondered when she would ever be able to catch up on her rest. And she was definitely not going to want to listen to any lies from Carl Silas when she got home. Bonnie was going to be too exhausted for any kind of husband and wife conversation. She did not want him to explain how he spent his time away from her. Her belief was that Carl Silas had a right to his privacy and so did she. Her values were important to her. She despised thieves, dope, ignorance, waste of natural resources, and obesity, among other things.

Bonnie picked up Night's body with plastic bags over her hands. She had a big mess to clean up. But her stadium blanket was huge. So Night had really only gushed blood on her very handy travel stadium blanket. She covered his body with more plastic bags and put it in the back of her car with anything else that had been touched by his blood. Then she changed into fresh clothes. Bonnie put her dirty shoes and clothes in a plastic bag.

She cleaned up what she could as she used her camping shovel, covered with a plastic bag, to scoop up and shuffle the dirt around. If there was a crime scene, Bonnie wanted all the details to be confusing. But she did not see any other bloody spills. So she got in her car and left. Bonnie used the bridge near Madison to cross into Kentucky. At Frankfort, Kentucky, she took I64 to I75, and drove south, straight into Georgia. Bonnie went to her favorite park and to the top of the park mountain.

Bert Night had startled her today. And she did not have much time to prepare. She pulled his body out of her car and wedged him between some emergency cardboard boxes that she kept in her car. Night was costing her a fortune in supplies. He had been a filthy dope dealer with the audacity to try to kill her. She used her sledge hammer to pound him into a black pulp. Then she tossed him down the side of the cliff that was over the river below.

He could not be identified. In Georgia, Bert Night would blend in with any other pounded to death Black man that had been tossed down the side of a mountain. That would have to suffice, because she was out of time. Bonnie burned everything in a park grill. And she was going to need an ax if she had any problems. She was really going to miss that ax until she bought a new one. Then she hurled the ax down into the river with a long throw.

Her professional athletic ability was also something that she had wanted to pursue as a career with a big income. But she had married Carl Silas, instead. The wife of Carl Silas was supposed to stay at home, at least most of the time. But she was using her agile skills in her efforts against the mafia control when Carl Silas thought that she was at home.

Bonnie was using as little time as possible because many people would be looking for Bert Night in a few hours. The car that he had driven today may not have belonged to him. She was depending on the idea that he did not tell anybody exactly what he had been doing today. Trouble was not something that she was looking for. But Night had pushed her with a time crunch. She had too much blood to worry about with his death, too much of a mess. And she may have been seen by someone while she been talking to him this morning.

Then she called Carl Silas because she was going to be later than usual tonight. She told him, "I am going to be a little later than usual. You know that I like to shop. Are you okay with this, with me coming home a little later tonight? Do you want me to stop and buy that mango facial peel that I told you about? You could just try it. You are great looking, no matter what you do. But that dead skin could just be peeled away with any wrinkles. You are always very lovable with or without any mango facial peel."

Carl Silas was not as concerned with wrinkles as she was. But she did try to pamper and spoil him. Bonnie always asked him before she would buy him anything. She would only buy his clothes after he had told her exactly what he wanted according to the specific size and color. Regardless of his personal care, she was never going to have any wrinkles. Bonnie would only want to look twenty years old even if she was as old as ninety.

She said that she could fry up a chicken, if he wanted to eat at about ten o'clock that night. He always wondered why her healthy attitude allowed her to prefer fried chicken to baked chicken. Bonnie always told him that she was a southern belle. And, that was why she coated the chicken with flour and black pepper.

"I will not have enough time to marinate the chicken in Louisiana hot sauce. But I will make some dipping sauce with sour cream and red peppers. I really miss you today. I love you so much right now. I feel so happy just to have you to talk to when I feel so alone," she told him while she was looking over her clothes for any signs of blood. That was as close to being a real relationship as she would get with all of the trade offs for happiness in her compromised life.

"Ten is fine," he told her.

"Anything special you want?"

"No. The refrigerator is full of food."

"Almond cookies?" she asked him.

"I just want almonds without the cookies. Less calories."

"We have lots of almonds. I will hurry home. I need to be close to you right now."

"Take your time. Drive safe. Love always."

"Always," she said and hung up the phone.

Bonnie checked her hands and everything for any visible signs of blood. She took a minute to relax and think about how things would be better for her now that Bert Night was dead. The Louisville Metro Police would not fall apart. But the cops, that Night was sending to kill her, would probably have less of an advantage. Maybe her dreams would now focus on Earl Mait. Her quiet sleep might now be filled with her lust to kill Earl Mait, Jefferson County Attorney. Mait as dead and gone would help a lot.

For a little while, she drove the long way back to home. The back roads were deserted. She could relax a little more because Bert Night was dead. And that made her think about her sister, Mindy Plumes. Mindy had always acted like Night. She was slimy. But Bonnie had not noticed those things about Mindy when Mindy was a little girl. She just thought that Mindy was like her, then. However, Mindy was not like Bonnie. Mindy was not so smart. And Mindy was completely evil.

Mindy Plumes was a dope dealer. Bonnie had not understood any of those things about Mindy. Much later, when Bonnie was older and had watched dope dealers at drug meets, she had recognized all those things about Mindy that meant that she was a dope dealer Mindy was always tapping her forefinger three times. Mindy would tap her forefinger once for a hit. That was what the dope dealers did.

Mindy was a lot shorter than Bonnie. And, at one time, she had a key to Bonnie's house. When Bonnie was in middle school, Mindy was always breaking things that belonged to Bonnie. Bonnie never really noticed it then. She just thought that those were accidents. But, there was nothing accidentally about Mindy. She was jealous of Bonnie and liked to try to turn Bonnie into a nothing kind of person.

Bonnie caught on somewhat, when she found Mindy sitting on Bonnie's sewing box. Bonnie kept her own scissors, clothes patterns, and supplies in her own sewing box. The lid on the sewing box had gotten cracked. And Bonnie had fixed the lid. Then one day, she had gone down to the basement and had seen Mindy sitting on the sewing box. So the lid on the sewing box had cracked again because Mindy weighed too much to sit on the box.

There was Mindy, talking on the phone and sitting on Bonnie's sewing box. Bonnie just stared at her. Then she had said, "Mindy, get off of it now. Right now."

"Off of what?" Mindy muttered.

"Off of my sewing box. Now."

"Sewing box?"

"Stop it, Mindy."

"Stop what?"

"Get off of my sewing box, now, you smart mouth trash."

"Move me."

"You are moved," Bonnie told her and knocked her off the sewing box.

"Keep your hands off of me."

"You keep your hands off of my things. You know that I fixed that. And you just broke it again."

"I am on the phone," Mindy said.

"You are on the floor. And if you get up, you are going to be on the floor again."

"I am on the phone. I can do anything that I want."

"If you get up, I will knock you down again. Dogs stay on the floor."

"Get off."

"Try to break my foot like you broke my sewing box, you little rat," Bonnie said.

Mindy stood up. And Bonnie slammed her back down onto the carpet. Mindy tried to stand up again. Bonnie knocked her back down. Then Bonnie put her foot on Mindy's chest and held her younger sister on the floor. Mindy was really angry. And Bonnie just held her there. Stepping on Mindy's face was what Bonnie really wanted to do, but her parents would probably object to that.

Then her mom came down into the basement and said, "What happened?"

"Bonnie will not get off of me," Mindy whined.

"Mindy keeps sitting on my sewing box, like a stool, and breaking the lid. I just fixed that lid two days ago. Mindy cracked it again," Bonnie said as she took her foot off of Mindy.

Her mom asked, "Why did you crack the lid, Mindy? Bonnie used the glue that Daddy bought for me, to fix that sewing box."

"I do not have to answer to you," Mindy sneered.

"Yes, Mindy. And you have to answer to me, too," Dad said as he came down the stairs. Then Bonnie went back up the stairs.

Mom and Dad just thought that Mindy was angry and fired up. But today, Bonnie knew that Mindy had probably been high. Mindy was always doing things like that at home. Once, Bonnie had come home and found Mindy in Bonnie's bedroom with the door locked. Bonnie had turned the knob and found that Mindy had locked the door. And Mom and Dad were not at home to stop the problem.

Then Bonnie knocked on the door and said, "Who is in my bedroom? Who locked this door?" Nobody answered. So Bonnie unlocked the door from the outside. And there inside was Mindy, standing in Bonnie's bedroom. She had been going through Bonnie's things. And Bonnie knew that Mindy had stolen Bonnie's change purse that Bonnie had thought was lost. That had been years ago. Mindy was supposed to be living somewhere in Shepherdsville, Kentucky now.

Mindy had probably stolen money from Mom and Dad, too. Mindy was incorrigible. Bonnie also had a pair of jeans and a shirt that was missing back then. She had put those dirty clothes in the laundry room. And the jeans and shirt just disappeared. Mindy was like a death row prisoner that did not care. She just kept pushing people around and stealing lots of things.

But Bonnie had thought that things were just getting lost and accidentally broken back then, too. She was completely astounded by such intense animal behavior from Mindy. She did not have any idea that people were so completely evil in such large groups, like dope gangs. Those were gangsters, drug dealing sociopaths. And Mindy was one of them.

When Bonnie was in grade school, she was always the one with the highest score in the class. Bonnie had just come to expect that she would be the one with the highest grade. If she had not gotten the highest grade, Bonnie would not have been crushed. She would just have wanted to know what she had done wrong.

But she never had thought about the other students that did not get the highest score. With Bonnie always being the best, the others always had to lose, be second best. Being busy with the Girl Scouts, the volleyball team, and the softball team, she was too young to understand how the other students might feel when they could not get that highest grade while they were competing with Bonnie. The other students would probably dislike Bonnie because they could not compete with her. Mindy could not compete with anybody in school because she was just average.

Strangely, Bonnie only wanted to help the other students. She wanted everybody to be great. She had a philosophy about life, that rationalized that people were mean when they were not happy. So she wanted everybody to be happy so that they would not bother her. Bonnie despised being annoyed and enjoyed learning. She like to read encyclopedias.

Her parents had two sets of encyclopedias for the kids. There was was the standard, regular set of encyclopedias, and a special set of encyclopedias about nature. The nature encyclopedias were about bugs and animals. Bonnie had read those books over and over. She thought that the pictures of the bugs and animals were great. Bonnie would catch a frog or a lightning bug, and then read about them again in the nature encyclopedia. And Mindy had never read the encyclopedias.

Bonnie was still deep in thought about Mindy when she took the ramp back onto the interstate highway so that she could get home. Bonnie always felt weird when she remembered about her grade school days. When she had realized that the other students had probably hated her, she had felt creepy. Her little friends, most likely, had not liked her at all. That could bring a tear to her eyes. She did like to have friends.

Bonnie had went to a Catholic grade school. She was a pretty little blonde girl that was always chosen to be in the procession to crown Mary. Bonnie wore fancy little dresses with the matching veils. She was a lovely little girl that would wear a blue or lilac dress for the procession. But the other little girls most likely had wanted to be in the procession, too. Bonnie always had a problem dealing with the jealousy of others. She just wanted to help. And Mindy just wanted to hurt people.

She remembered being in a spelling bee way back then. Bonnie was always in the spelling bees. The students would speak into a microphone when they were spelling. Bonnie was given the word paid. She spoke clearly and slowly into the microphone, "Paid. P-A-Y-E-D. Paid." The judge said that Bonnie had spelled the word wrong. And Bonnie had sat down.

When Bonnie had gotten home, her mom was upset. Mom said, "Oh, Bonnie. You spelled the word wrong. You did not win. Were you hurt?" Her mom made it sound like Bonnie was just always supposed to win.

When she went home, Bonnie had looked the word up in the dictionary. There were the words, paid and payed, which sounded the same. "The word has two different spellings which are both correct. P-A-I-D. And, P-A-Y-E-D. I was not hurt, Mom. That was just a contest. But I knew that I had seen that word in books and it was spelled, P-A-Y-E-D. What should we do, now?" Bonnie asked her mom.

"Call the school. Have a re-match?" her mom suggested.

"I do not want a re-match. It was just a contest. Not a college scholarship. But, we should tell somebody that I was correct."

"I will call the school now."

"The spelling bee was being recorded. So, the recording will be enough to explain what had happened," Bonnie said.

The next day in school Bonnie's teacher told the class that Bonnie had spelled the word correct. Bonnie could almost feel the anger from the class, and not because Bonnie had lost with a wrong judgment. The class had been waiting for Bonnie to be wrong. Bonnie had felt cold chills cover her when she had realized that her little friends were not her little friends at all. The class had enjoyed watching her lose. Bonnie had not even noticed that not one person had told her that they were sorry that she had not won the spelling bee. Mindy liked to watch Bonnie lose, too.

Bonnie was like a tumbleweed back then. She liked to observe everything and read everything. And she really wanted to have friends. Mom and Dad had wanted her to have friends, too. Bonnie was involved in everything. But, she did not have too many friends. She played with the neighborhood kids. And, her friends from grade school were only the kids that liked to be friends with the highest scorer in the class.

The odd part was that Bonnie had lots of self-confidence. She was conceited and hated to be wrong. Bonnie was not angry when people did not like her. She just wondered why they would want to spend time with her while they were only jealous of her. She was a trusting person that would always move on in her life because she was always thinking about space travel, new inventions, and being extremely wealthy.

When she went into the Advanced Placement program in high school, Bonnie was happier. All the Advanced Placement students were the ones that made the other students lose. Now, with the rest of the gifted, high I.Q. students in their own class with Bonnie, the other students in the other classes could compete with each other. The same student would not win with the highest test score each time.

Bonnie was not like the usual bookworm student. She was adventurous. In grade school she had wanted to be in everything. She had sung in the school plays, had played on the school teams, and had wanted to take art classes after school. Mom had said no to the art classes while Bonnie was still so young. Bonnie just wanted to learn everything. If Bonnie knew that there was a class, then Bonnie wanted to learn that subject. And Mindy hated to have to even read a book.

So, it was no surprise, that when Bonnie had heard about cheerleading in grade school, she just went to the try outs before her Little Brownie meeting. Bonnie watched the other kids doing their try out cheer without really listening. She did not want to be late for the Little Brownie meeting. So, she had just got up in front of the group and had did her cheer for the try outs when they had called her name.

Everybody just stared at her. And, then she just sat down again. One of the older girls walked over to Bonnie and told her that she had done the wrong cheer. Bonnie did not know that there was a cheer for the try outs. She had just seen the notice on the board and went to the try outs after school. Bonnie did not know what she was supposed to do for the try outs. She had watched the two other students before her. Then, when it was Bonnie's turn, she walked out in front of the group and did an impromptu cheer that she had made up while she was standing up there. Mindy would never get up in front of an audience for any reason.

And Bonnie had not even cared that she had just walked in front of a crowd of people, had done something completely wrong, had made up her own cheer, had not done the same cheer that every other kid was supposed to do for the try out, and was only wondering how she could be a cheerleader. The older girl had showed her how to do the correct cheer. After Bonnie had learned the new cheer, in just a few minutes, then she had done that new cheer for the try out group. But, Bonnie was still not chosen for the cheerleading squad. And Mindy liked it that Bonnie was not picked to be a cheerleader.

So, she was not a cheerleader in grade school. What bothered her about that whole thing, was that not one person had told her about the cheer that she had needed to learn for the try outs. Losing out on being on the cheerleading squad was just something else that Bonnie had added to her grade school experience. She still had got to learn how to try out for cheerleading. So, she had lost being on the squad. Bonnie just like to try and learn things.

Mindy had never done any of those things. And Bonnie had never noticed that back then. Bonnie was just doing what Bonnie wanted to do and assuming that Mindy was doing whatever Mindy wanted to do. When Bonnie had gotten older, and thought about those grade school kids, she had been even more happy about her Advanced Placement experience. She liked being smart and noticed that Mindy was stupid.

Once when the toilet had clogged while Mindy was in the bathroom at her parents house, Mindy had stood there holding the flush handle up on the toilet tank, while the water was almost going to flood the floor. Bonnie had pushed Mindy out of the way and turn off the water to the toilet. Then, Bonnie had plunged the toilet with the plunger and loosened the clog. Mindy really was dumb. She was a typical dope trash person. And, Mindy had probably been flushing something down the toilet that she did not want Mom to find. One of Mindy's friends, Weedhopper, was always smoking marijuana back then, as Bonnie was later told.

After Bonnie had bought her own house, she had left spare keys with Mom and Dad for emergencies. One morning after working her third shift job, Bonnie had come home and found Mindy with one of her girlfriends, Betty. Each of the girls were sleeping on one of Bonnie's two loveseats. Bonnie had stood there and stared at those two girls in her house. Mindy had never asked Bonnie if they could sleep there because she knew that Bonnie would not want them in her house. Bonnie woke them up by shouting, "Get out! Get out now, Mindy. Go out the door, Betty. Wake up and get out."

Both girls sat up and stared at Bonnie. With the same blank look on their faces, they did not know where they were and stared in confusion. Bonnie said again, "Get out Mindy. Go home Betty. Out of my house, now."

"Bonnie," was all that Mindy said.

Betty whined, "What time is it?"

"It is time for you to leave my home, Mindy and Betty. Get out now."

"Do you see my shoes, Bonnie? Mindy put them somewhere. And, I could not find them," Betty replied.

"You are in my house without permission, Betty. Now, get out. I do not care if you have to walk barefoot in the snow. This is my house. Mine. Get out. I am tired. Now, get out," Bonnie told her coldly.

"She is never going to let you have a horse here, Mindy. She just threw us out of her house. Where are my shoes?" Betty asked.

"Your shoes are in the car, Betty. Bonnie give her some shoes so that we can get out of here and go home," Mindy declared.

"I am not giving Betty any of my shoes. Now get out. There is not a car in the driveway. So, however you got here, you can just walk home. And, do not come back. Leave now. And, I am going to check your pockets before you leave," Bonnie said stronger.

"You stay off of me, Bonnie," Mindy told her.

"You stay out of my house, Mindy. Now try to keep me off. I am checking your pockets. You are a little nut. But, you are not my little nut. You are leaving and not taking any of my things with you. Mindy, you are a loser. You can not just come into my home like you used to go in and out of my bedroom when I lived with Mom and Dad. This is my home, you scummy little crumb of dirt," Bonnie informed her. And Bonnie searched both of them.

As Mindy was walking by Bonnie, so that she could go out of the door, she waved her hand, back and forth, in front of Bonnie's face. Then she snarled at Bonnie, "What are you going to do about that? How are you going to stop that? Like you own the world."

Bonnie shoved Mindy against the wall, grabbed Mindy's hand and pushed it up over her head. Then she grabbed Mindy's other hand and pushed it up over Mindy's head, too. Bonnie held both of Mindy's hands there, while she stepped on both of Mindy's feet. While Mindy was held in place, Bonnie grabbed the skin across Mindy's abdomen and started to twist Mindy's skin.

Bonnie breathed the words very slowly at Mindy, "Like this, Mindy. So do not even think about spitting on me. I can just twist your skin ever so slowly. Make it feel like a pair of pliers cutting into your flesh. You see, Mindy, this is my home. You came looking for a fight. I told you to stop it. I can also back it up. I have a life that does not include you. I do not want your problems. You are a mean little person that I found in my home without my permission. Mindy, you just like to hurt people. You started it. Now get out." And Bonnie pushed Mindy toward the front door.

Bonnie watched both of them leave her property. Betty walked out into the cold without any shoes. And Betty continued walking down Bonnie's driveway, and only started running when she reached the street, probably because her feet had started freezing. Mindy just kept walking with a disoriented saunter. Those two girls were weird and probably high on dope.

Then Bonnie changed the lock on her back door with her spare lock, bolted the other doors closed, and went to the hardware store to buy new locks. She changed the locks and went to sleep thinking about what Mindy and Betty might have done while they were in her home. They could not have stolen any of her cash because her desk was locked.

She thought that they had probably gone through everything in her house. Then, they had fallen asleep on her furniture. Bonnie was livid. She thought about how Mindy has asked Bonnie if she would let her keep a horse on her back lot. Mindy, incredibly worthless Mindy, wanted Bonnie to keep a horse for her on her property. Mindy thought that Bonnie was supposed to build a barn, buy a horse, pay for a veterinarian, and keep a horse for Mindy.

Bonnie did not even like to talk to Mindy, much less, keep a horse for her. That is why Bonnie was happy at Christmas after her parents had both died. Bonnie never had to see her family again. She had always hated Christmas, but had to come home for Christmas because of Mom and Dad.

And, Bonnie thought about what Mindy might have done if Bonnie had a husband. Mindy was really bad in that way as Bonnie remembered. Once when the family had gone to the lake, Bonnie had asked her boyfriend if he wanted to go waterskiing. Bonnie showed up later than expected at the lake. When Bonnie got there, she found out that Mindy had taken Randy, Bonnie's boyfriend, out on the boat.

Then, she had been told by everybody else that had also been on the boat, that Mindy had decided to stretch out under the sun. Mindy had been resting on her stomach when she had asked Randy to untie the back of her swimsuit top so that she would not have a tan line. Randy had untied the swimsuit top while everybody just stared. Then, Mindy had asked Randy to rub suntan lotion on her back. So Dad had told Randy that he would put the lotion on Mindy's back.

Dad said quietly, "Mindy that is Bonnie's boyfriend. You have to stop it. You fight with Bonnie all the time. That man likes Bonnie. She is a tall smart, blonde. You are shorter with dark hair. For a very long time you have been trying to make Bonnie miserable. This got a lot worse when you did not pass the Advanced Placement test. We had you tested because you wanted to be in the program like Bonnie. That was high school, Mindy. You were not smart enough."

Then, he tied the back of her swimsuit top. Dad continued softly with, "Keep your swimsuit top tied. You can do something with your life. And, you will do something faster if you stop spending so much time trying to get even with Bonnie for being smart. Bonnie has enough energy for ten people. And, she just dreams all the time about the future with new things. That is Bonnie. You need to take time to find out what Mindy wants, and to concentrate on that. Now, just stop making the problem worse. I married your Mom because I liked your Mom. Randy likes to be with Bonnie, not with you. And, Bonnie will not just let it slide when she hears about you coming on to Randy. Now, stop it now. The fight will happen anyway because you already did it." Dad had let the fight happen between Bonnie and Mindy so that Mindy might learn something about how people would not put up with her trying to mess up their lives.

That was how Mindy acted when she got older. She liked to win. But, Mindy could only win by getting rid of the better person. Mindy was really less than average. She would not try to find her unique talent because her time was always spent making trouble for other people. Worthless human being, was how Bonnie described Mindy, even when she was very young.

So, the rosary was probably something that Mindy had done, too. When Bonnie was in the fifth grade, she had found a very pretty rosary in her drawer, with her socks. Bonnie took the rosary to her Mom to ask her why she had put it with her socks.

Mom said, "That is Grandma's rosary. Wonder why she put it your drawer?"

"Maybe she wanted me to have it," Bonnie said.

"If Grandma wanted you to have it, she would have handed it to you. I will call Grandma and ask her right now. We will find out how it got there."

"Grandma knows that I am in the procession for the crowning of Mary."

"Yes, Bonnie. But, I think that somebody else took Grandma's rosary and put it in your drawer."

As Bonnie was driving back home from Georgia today, remembering all those things from so long ago, she was pretty sure that Mindy had taken Grandma's rosary and put it in Bonnie's drawer. One of the things that could have happened, would have been that Mom and Dad would have thought that Bonnie had stolen the rosary from Grandma.

Grandma had just told Mom that she could not find the rosary. Grandma had also said that the rosary had probably gotten tangled up with the laundry. And then Grandma had said that she guessed that the rosary had probably gotten washed and put away with Bonnie's socks.

Bonnie thought that Mindy had probably been doing vicious things like that, all of her life. And Mindy had gotten worse after Mom and Dad had died because by then, there was absolutely nobody that wanted to help Mindy. That Bonnie just wanted to stay away from Mindy, was the way that Bonnie explained things to Carl Silas. The truth was that Bonnie hated Mindy in the same way that Bonnie hated all dope dealers. Mindy had probably ruined lots of lives. But, Mindy, the dope dealer, could be traced to Bonnie too easily for Bonnie to actually do anything about Mindy.

Bonnie kept her distance from Mindy while Bonnie was doing what she could. Mindy was a problem that Bonnie knew about, like the rest of the problems that included Earl Mait, the dope dealing Jefferson County Attorney, that had given the mafia the control of the city. Bonnie felt her anger rising again, as she always did when she could not get close enough to stop a problem.

She wanted to push the dope dealing mafia out and also knew that the mafia would never leave. But there had to be some places that they could still keep safe by not letting in the dope dealers. Bonnie would always fight and kill the dope dealers. But now, she had to get home and to avoid having any fights with her husband, Carl Silas.

Chapter 4   More Family

Carl Silas called Bonnie, at her office, to tell her that Wallace Joseph was coming to live with them. He was excited because Wally Joe had been a C.P.A. for years, and was now going to go to medical school. Both of them had wanted to go at the same time. But, Wally Joe was not accepted when Carl Silas started medical school. Bonnie let that sink in for a minute, noticing that Carl Silas had over looked the fact that she had been terrorized by drug dealers, infected with hookworms, and missed out on medical school, even though she was still trying to be admitted.

She spoke softly, "Sounds great. Another doctor in the family. We have plenty of room, lots of food, and could use the company."

He noticed her gentle reply and said, "I know that you want to go to medical school. I want to start a family, too. Wally Joe will be good company."

Bonnie avoided that for a minute. Then she said, "That is what marriage is for, families. When is Wally Joe coming?" Never mind the fact that she only wanted to move away, to leave. And the only reason that she stayed here was because Carl Silas gave her a source of protection and safety. If she found a better husband with more money, in a better part of the world, then she would be gone.

Her husband almost shouted, "Tonight. He was looking for a place to stay. He already resigned from his partnership, but that is just paperwork. His money is in the business. I told him to just come. We will have a great time. Right?"

Bonnie talked softer, "Only the best. We will have more family with us." She was always polite to Carl Silas. They never fought. She did not want to fight. Peace, safety, and comfort, those were the things what Bonnie wanted. Wally Joe just would be another person to navigate around. She would have to be even more careful when Wally Joe came to live with them. Her husband's brother had never even really spent any time getting to know her because she liked to stay apart from other people.

Believing that Carl Silas was in love with her, or at least wanted her a lot, gave Bonnie a little leeway with her part in the efforts against the drug dealers. She made her husband happy so that there would not be any conflicts for her to deal with at home. Carl Silas was content around her and happy enough not to notice too much about her. She never gave him any reason to wonder about what she might be doing.

Tonight, she would race through the grocery store after she left the office. She told Meredith, her dental assistant, that Wally Joe was staying with them and that he may come by the office. That was enough for Meredith to know.

Bonnie got home very fast, with only an hour lost for the trip to the grocery. That gave her some more time alone to think about different things. She just grabbed food from the shelves until her shopping cart was full. Then she piled the food in bags as she used the self-service check out. If she shopped more, she could have more time alone. Her husband was really spending too much time with her at home.

Earlier, when she had called, Carl Silas had answered the phone seriously. She had wanted to tell him that she would be late. "Hi, Sweetheart. I am going to go buy Wally Joe some groceries. We can eat what he does not want. I will put them in the refrigerator in the laundry room," she said.

Her breathing was a little tight. So, she took a quick breath and swallowed. Then, she added, "I will move my home office refrigerator into his room until the new appliances arrive. We can fix it up with his choice of appliances. The rooms will make a nice apartment. I always stay at a hotel when I visit somebody. I need the privacy. And Wally Joe will be safe with us and want to stay longer with an apartment of his own. We could order from Sears online tonight. What do you think? I will be just a little later than usual."

"Order online. Sears has appliances with great features, too. Just cheaper, not as classy. I will ask Wally Joe when I get home. I want him to be a part of all decisions. He will be comfortable, fast and easy. You are great with organization and details," he warmly said.

"And, that room opens onto the patio. If we just change the lock, Wally Joe can have a private entrance from the patio. Okay? Does Wally Joe have any special likes or dislikes? I mean like fabric softener or tea. I want to make him happy for you," Bonnie perked out with gusto. She was enjoying the project of Wally Joe and the apartment because he could just choose the appliances.

"Wally Joe likes you, that much I have been told. I have stolen one of his lady athletes. And he was not pleased, since he did win all of them from me, with an arm wrestling match. I told him to ask me for more clothes if he need any. You never know how to dress until get somewhere. He will be a medical school student. Money is low for them. So, I told him he could always use one of our cars. We have the four wheel drive, out back that we only drive sometimes. And, I said that I would just buy a new one for him to use, if that was not good enough. He should only have to worry about school. And, we could ask him if he wants to borrow some more money with a loan from us. Or, we could just give him $10,000 or so. He needs to finish school. And, stay in shape. If our equipment is not good enough, we could get him a membership at a twenty-four hour gym. We will talk to him. And, order from Sears, tonight. Be careful. And, may I please have some of those Hawaiian Sweet Rolls in the safety sealed package. A package for Wally Joe, too. I feel like we are taking care of our kids with him being here. Maybe, by next year, we will have one of our own. Love and drive safely," he added as he hung up the phone. Someone must have walked in because he ended the call quickly.

She grabbed the groceries that she had bought in the reusable shopping bags. Those bags were great for travelers. She could give them to Wally Joe. That would be one less thing that he would need to ask for from her. As she was walking in the house, Wally Joe met her at the back door.

"So, Wally Joe, which bedroom would you like. You are a long time guest, so pick where you want to stay," Bonnie offered.

"Downstairs. No questions about it. The room in the back," Wally Joe answered.

"That room has an adjoining room, so we will just go ahead and add the extras, to make it into a small apartment. We were going to do it, anyway. Now, you can pick the microwave, washer, and dryer. Just go by the store. Then, we will have them delivered. The hook ups are installed. And, get any other appliances you want delivered. Make yourself at home. Then, you will not need anything. Refrigerator, too. Do you need a food processor? Make the whole thing spectacular. Privacy will keep you here, safe with us," Bonnie said.

"Groceries, Wally Joe. Take what you want. We will put them away in the laundry room refrigerator. And, I will move my small home office refrigerator into your room until the appliances arrive. I will put about five different meals into the oven for you tonight. Fried chicken, catfish, pork chops, beef lasagna, spinach lasagna. Okay? Now, you will feel at home. We usually eat late because of my office hours. And Carl Silas decided to teach evening classes," she assured him.

"Carl Silas told me. I think Sears will be fine. I can cook for myself. But, I would never turn down a home cooked meal from a beautiful woman. I could use a refrigerator in the room tonight. Carl Silas said that you have a furniture dolly in the laundry room. I can move the refrigerator myself," he responded.

She had dinner on the table in a little more than thirty minutes. The cottage cheese salad had chunks of fresh, sliced tomatoes, green pepper rings, sliced onions, and grated sharp cheddar cheese. Baked potatoes with sour cream, green beans with garlic sauce, fried corn with onions, catfish, biscuits, and pecan ice cream, completed the meal. Bonnie skipped the ice cream and went to move the refrigerator.

Wally Joe and Carl Silas would probably keep talking for hours. She put the refrigerator in Wally Joe's room. Then, she went to the Sears website and printed out the best appliances online. Bonnie knew that she could get into a hot, bubble bath, really soon, if she worked fast. A notepad for Wally Joe to write down anything that he needed was left by their kitchen refrigerator. She took the print outs of the Sears appliances to them, so Wally Joe could decide what he wanted to use.

"Never mind about the dishes. Which appliances do you want? Just circle them," she said. The refrigerator had an ice maker. Wally Joe liked the chrome surface, but decided on white for everything, so that all the appliances would match.

"That will be enough for you? There is more floor space for more things, if you want more things," Carl Silas told Wally Joe.

"With the lock for the patio door, my private entrance, and these appliances, what else would I need? I believe that is more than enough," Wally Joe piped up.

"Well. Let us add another key lock to the inside door for your bedroom. Then, you can lock us out of your apartment. We have some new locks that were going to use for the new garage doors. Change the locks again if you want. Just keep talking to Carl Silas. And I will go and order the Sears online," Bonnie said sweetly.

She ordered the Sears appliances. And she got next day delivery for the appliances. Then she changed the locks for Wally Joe. Finally the time had come, and Bonnie went upstairs to run the hot bath water. When she came back downstairs, she put the food away, the dishes in the sink, rinsed them off, loaded the dishwasher, and headed back upstairs through the dining room.

"The refrigerator is in your room Wally Joe. Both locks are changed. The appliances will be left on the back porch tomorrow. I can hook them up. There are more snacks and potato chips in the kitchen. The dishes are done. Remember to use anything that you want, Wally Joe. And Carl Silas, I am headed for a hot bubble bath while you two talk the night away," she said as she kissed Carl Silas on her way out of the room.

"You can not just leave after all that work," Wally Joe told her as he grabbed her to hug her tight.

Bonnie just looked at Carl Silas. His face lost the smile and gained a serious look. Then his eyes smiled again. "Wally Joe we got you everything, but a woman. That is my wife. But, even I will admit that she does look good on you," Carl Silas said as he laughed.

"That is why I picked the women athletes. Those are the woman that go well with my eyes and smile," Wally Joe replied.

"Now, that we have been thanked. May the adornment leave for her bath? I look good on lots of people. And time is fleeting," she pleaded. She unwrapped herself from Wally Joe and left the room.

"I did not think that you would let go of her that fast, Wally Joe," Carl Silas said, as he stared him down.

"I will hold any woman as long as I want, even your wife, Carl Silas," Wally Joe uttered softly.

Carl Silas spoke even softer, "Now! Put it down." He put his arm on the table.

"Yes. Now," Wally Joe spoke back.

They arm wrestled for a long time until Wally Joe won. Then Carl Silas, got him in a head lock and tossed him unto the dining room carpet. He pinned him in a wrestling hold and pulled off his shoes and socks. Then Carl Silas, tickled his feet until he laughed so hard at Wally Joe that he lost his grip. And Wally Joe held up his arms in surrender.

But, Carl Silas picked up a biscuit from the table and hit him in the face. Carl Silas was becoming more angry because Wally

Joe was always being told to stay away from other men's wives. And, Wally Joe did not care what the other men might say to him. However, Carl Silas believed that Bonnie would ignore anything unusual from Wally Joe.

Then Wally Joe lunged at Carl Silas with a tackle. He sat on Carl Silas on the dining room floor.

"No more wrestling. No more food fights. I came to study," Wally Joe instructed his brother.

"And to hold my wife. Right in front of my eyes," Carl Silas reprimanded Wally Joe.

"You were never jealous before about any woman. But, you never married one before, either. So, we will set a standard for your wife. If I can take her, then I will. And, then the apartment will be yours, Carl Silas," he challenged.

"I have decided to trust you because you are my brother. When I do not trust you, I will throw you out. Then Mother will want to know why I threw you out. And, I will tell her that you tried to take my wife away from me. Maybe, Christmas will be without you, then. So, stop it. Now, do you want me to buy a new car for you to use? Do you want me to give you about $10,000, or co-sign a loan? Do you need to wear or keep any of my clothes? That woman will always stay with me. She is my wife, the future mother of my children," Carl Silas promised him.

Wally Joe said, "You still have your mighty ego. Yes. I would like to use a show room new car. Cash would be fine. Now, I need to look through the groceries."

"Everything is put away. She is absolutely great. And, she has been applying to medical schools, too. Things were not so good for her for a little while," Carl Silas confided.

"So, we can talk longer, then. I want to ask you some questions, anyway," he told him.

"We can talk about her because I want you to be nice, very nice, extremely nice to my wife. She had great parents, but slimy siblings. She does not have any contact with them. Her parents are dead. Her sister, and there was more than one of them, was a nightmare of behavior. Bonnie learned to sew and to tailor clothing in grade school. Then, she decided to make a coat. She bought a pattern, fabric, buttons, and lining. She worked on the coat. Finished up a completely lined coat, just like off a store rack. Her sister used a black marker to ruin the back of the coat when the coat was put in the laundry basket. Bonnie just threw the coat away," Carl Silas told Wally Joe. He poured another cup of coffee for himself, then went on talking to his brother.

"And once, when she was going down the stairs to the basement, she saw her sister as she was talking on the phone and sitting on top of Bonnie's sewing basket. The sewing basket had cracked somehow, before. And, Bonnie had fixed it with glue. Her sister had used that sewing basket for a stool and broken it. Then, she sat on it and broke it again, after Bonnie had fixed it. Bonnie tried to succeed all the time, but they held her back with their trouble.

She absolutely never speaks with any of them, not any contact, not at all," he told Wally Joe directly.

Wally Joe stared at him. Then he said, "I would just hold her until the hurt went away. And, we could have our own Christmas."

"She is only helping you. And she is very serious and will not find your jokes and antics amusing. Bonnie is athletic, but not an air head idiot. You would be abrasive to her. She likes to read and to do research. You could lose her as a friend if you push her. She is not made of iron. But, our home is safe and protected enough for her," Carl Silas answered.

"What I wanted to know was if I could just ensconce myself in the apartment. I have not been to classes for a long time. This is your home, but I want alone time. Not to hang out with you," Wally Joe replied seriously.

"That is what Bonnie said, too. She keeps trying for more. The two of you are alike with the same need to get something else out of life. But, she is not selfish. Bonnie takes care of the little things first, and quickly, to leave time for more. We thought that you might like a membership to a twenty-four hour gym to keep you focused. Mostly, what my home is, is safe," Carl Silas added.

"I never say no to a gift. Can we sleep, now? My day was long," Wally Joe said.

Carl Silas smiled and offered, "Sleep. Yes. But, we will have a marathon conversation, eventually, so you can tell me why you, with all your women, are still not married."

"Deal. And, good night," Wally Joe ended.

They left the dining room without seeing Bonnie standing in the kitchen doorway. She had watched Carl Silas hit his brother with a biscuit and wrestle on the floor. That was not how the intense and serious husband, that Bonnie knew, usually acted around her. She had just stood there wearing a bath towel under her robe as she thought about how her husband acted so very differently with his brother.

She had heard the noise, thought that there was a problem, and came to find two brothers playing. Bonnie heard Carl Silas say that Wally Joe chased women. She was going to say something, but did not want to spoil the close bonding of the moment. She could almost touch the emotions in the air. It was not really like spying when she had just stood there, because she had come to help. Then they had left before she could say anything.

She went back to her bath and to wait for her husband. The bath water was still warm when her toes felt the bubbles again. Turning on the hot water, she let bathroom fill with steam. She rubbed coconut oil in her hair and on her face. Her thoughts were heavy with fear as she considered that perhaps Carl Silas was more aware of her isolated life. Bonnie believed that she had him pampered into oblivion.

She soaked for just a few minutes more. Carl Silas should not be alone until he was asleep. And with Wally Joe in the house, she would have to be more careful about wandering around the house at night after her husband was asleep. When she finally went and snuggled in the bed, she was so tired that she slept until morning.

While she was sleeping, two truckers in the Louisville river port area found two dope dealers parked nearby after they had dropped their loads. The truckers walked behind the cars carrying some broken pallet boards. When the dope dealers got out of their cars, the truckers just pounded them to death. Then they threw the bloody boards into some nearby weeds, spit on the drug dealers, and said, "We truck, Louisville." The truckers smiled at each other and left with their trucks.

Bonnie was still groggy with sleep, when she was listening to Wally Joe, the next morning. "You are great. I never thought that Carl Silas would marry an athletic woman. I was always attracted to the sports women. And, Carl Silas, he was always looking at the models. You look good, work out, and organize things super. With all that going for you, Carl Silas, even says that you are a fantastic cook," Wally Joe smiled back.

"And, a dentist. Carl Silas likes smart woman, too. I wanted to go to medical school like you. But, things happened. Still, I believe that my evening appointment hours allow for a difference. People should not have to take off from work, or take the kids out of school, so that they can go to a dentist. I have been applying to medical schools since I got my license. Research is what I like. Root canal therapy is prehistoric. They used to pull the tooth because they could not control the infection with the root canal problem. Now, they open up the tooth. File and clean inside. Then, fill the tooth with rubber so it will not get infected again," she lamented.

"Like cancer, when they would just amputate a limb," he commented.

"Yes. I want to make a micro hole into the tooth, remove the infected material, and then, treat the infection. Arestin, triple antibiotic, whatever works," Bonnie bounced back.

"Reasonable. I have to do my time before I can do research. C.P.A., that career did not offer me much in the biological sciences. You, however, do have a science background. And, Carl Silas, he beat both of us. I had to tag on my science courses outside of my regular classes. That was many years ago. But, I will like medicine better," he said longingly.

Then he looked her right in the eye, and said, "I need to get one of you. Same size, color, and personality. Carl Silas has always known that the athletic women are mine. We arm wrestled for them once. I won. And, I am not going to let him cut into my action. You see I like the way that my arm fits around their shoulders like this." And then, he put his arm around her.

Bonnie was used to men. She liked them a lot. So, she just leaned into his hold. Then she said, "Now, I know what you feel like. I will definitely know the difference if I run into you and not Carl Silas in the dark."

And she stepped away from him slowly and said, "Okay. Time is flying. You can grab what you want from the house for your apartment. But we will have to go to a store eventually, for all of it. However, I will guess that you have things to do for now. So we will make you comfortable for your first few nights. Do you want some bubble bath? I have a clove fragrance that is really woodsy. Make a list of anything."

She handed him a notepad. And she added, "I never select for anyone. I buy what you tell me. Even an egg flipper for a fry pan should be your choice in style and color."

He smiled deceptively, put his arm around her shoulder again, and said, "Like I said, Carl Silas invaded my share of the women when he married you. You are a perfect fit, right there."

"I fit perfectly in lots of places. Now, I need to fit perfectly in my car and go to the office. Use what you want, what you need. The house is yours. Have to go," Bonnie said and patted his arm.

She left the house without a friendly sister-in-law to brother-in-law kiss. Bonnie was not going to be offended by any playful roughhousing from Wally Joe. But, she had never tested this in front of Carl Silas. So a kiss on the cheek might be the wrong thing to do at this time, since Wally Joe was not that shy.

Her most important objective was to never fight with Carl Silas. Wally Joe could fight with Carl Silas as much as he wanted. And apparently, he did not care how much they did or did not fight. Carl Silas had never been married before. Now one of them had a wife, to place between the two of them. And she was not going to be a trophy for their battles. Her husband was supposed to be the part of her life that was without any problems.

Traffic was slow on her way to the office. She was trying to decide how to deal with Wally Joe. The apartment, fully furnished would keep him separate. His being apart from them, was better for her. Having Wally Joe too close would be a definite problem. She was just imagining how Wally Joe could create problems by keeping track of her.

She had just been coming out of the nearly empty store yesterday, in Paris, Kentucky, and onto the empty side parking lot, when she saw the trucker hit the guy from behind. Before that, he had told the guy to wait right there while he went to get something on the other side of the trailer. Then four more men walked back around with the first trucker.

He snarled at the guy, "You told that cop to stop those two trucks on I64, in Louisville, and to give the drivers false tickets. You run the dope for a band of filth. And, your misfits wanted to rifle those commercial driver licenses from those truckers so that you could take their jobs. From the slums, you go around making trouble for other people, so that you can wipe them out. What are going to do with their stuff in your ghetto, after you steal it? Use their tools to play with mud pies? That was my brother that you hit, trash."

The trucker hit the guy hard on the side of the head. Then he said, "Where is your cop with my ticket? Can you tell him it was me?" The trucker banged the guy on the other side of his head.

One of the other guys said, "He was not your brother, Smokey Ribs"

"He could have been my brother, if my mother had another boy. I say that he was. Because I hate this weasel," Smokey Ribs said as he hit the dope dealer in the abdomen. The dope dealer was afraid and did not move. But there was no gang beating, because only Smokey Ribs pounded him. Bonnie knew that the dope dealer was not going to walk away from this. The other guys would carry his body. Smokey Ribs knocked him around to the other side of the trailer that was parked behind the store. Bonnie saw Smokey Ribs beat and kicked him.

Then the dope dealer started to fight back and tried to run away. "Get off of me," the dope dealer yelled. Smokey Ribs swelled up when the dope dealer tried to run.

One of the other guys said, "Talk pretty big when you have a cop to write false tickets for you. You are just a mean rag doll that ruins the lives of others. We are not going to die for your benefit. We like it the other way. We want it the other way. You die."

Smokey Ribs grabbed the dope dealer and slammed him against the concrete block wall. Then he picked up a broken board from a pallet. That dope dealer was beaten to death. Then, they picked him up on a wood pallet and took him away.

That was when Bonnie had walked to her car so that she could drink her orange juice while it still cold. She had just stopped because she had drank all of her water while she was eating crackers with hot sauce.

At times like that, Wally Joe could definitely make a problem for her if he was around too much. Her people seethed with hate. Their lives were destroyed and would never be replaced. When they had lost their jobs at the car plant because of the gangs, they were in serious trouble because they did not have college training. They came from trade schools and apprentice programs, and went into manufacturing jobs. With benefits, jobs at the car plant could pay enough to buy a two-story house with a two car garage on a couple of acres. They still had their bills to pay after their jobs were gone.

A forty hour work week, at about twenty-five dollars an hour, could mean getting paid about one thousand dollars each week. When they had to go from earning about one thousand dollars each week, to earning nothing, they had to make big adjustments. And because they had been fired as a result of lies from dope dealers, the company had no intention of letting them draw unemployment benefits. The state of Kentucky did not really pay unemployment benefit checks any more because the companies would make false charges against the fired employees. So Smokey Ribs did not really have any other option for protecting his job, except to kill the dope dealer, since the gangs ran everything.

Those thoughts of yesterday drifted away, as she finally arrived at her office. Bonnie was always proud of her second shift hours. Sometimes, she felt completely alone with her need for a better world. Second shift office hours gave her more patients and some free mornings. She found out that people did like to come to the dentist during the evenings more than on Saturdays. That way, they could keep their off day, Saturday, free for other things.

And Bonnie liked to come in on Saturdays, too. She had always like to work the weekends. If Carl Silas would find something to do on Sundays, then she would also offer Sunday office hours. The weekends were quiet and less crowded. Bonnie would scan the Internet, send emails, and read when she did not have a patient in the office. She was working on her brochures on how to keep your mouth clean and your teeth free from cavities.

Tonight, she only had one patient at eight o'clock, unless another one had called for an appointment. Her website needed more work and more information, so she worked on it. The printer in the office could print anything for the patient from her website. But, she still wanted to set out a few printed brochures on swishing your mouth with water and chewing sugarless gum with xylitol.

She thought that dentures were for people that had birth defects. If a person had been born without teeth, or had been born with a deformed mouth, then dentures could help these unfortunate people. But, Bonnie wanted everybody that had teeth, to keep their teeth for life.

David arrived at seven o'clock, very early for his appointment that evening. Bonnie asked him if he wanted to start early because she was not with another patient. David said that he wanted to look over her website for a few minutes before the appointment. He had a few questions that he wanted to ask her.

"Just come to the window when you are ready. If you need a notepad and pen, there are some on the desk. Take your time and print what you like," she told him. Then Bonnie went back to writing her brochures.

At seven-thirty, David said that he was ready. He got in the examination chair with his notes. He was looking really good in his blue shirt and jeans.

She asked him, "What do you want to know?"

"About fluoride. I think that I need more," David said.

"Fluoride comes in different percentages in the many brands of toothpastes. If you want more fluoride, just read the labels. You can also get a prescription toothpaste with more fluoride than the regular toothpastes. Fluoride is protected by law because it can have side effects. But fluoride is important for protecting your teeth from decay. Mostly, you also need to keep your mouth clean. Food rots in your mouth, bacteria forms, sugars and acids attack your teeth. I will try to post a list of toothpastes with their fluoride percentages on my website. Teeth do not have to decay. What else?" she asked him.

"That was really it. I noticed how you tried to group the information on the website. Dentures are not what I want, not at all," he answered.

"David, I do not want anybody to be forced to wear dentures. I want you to have your teeth for the rest of your life. Treatment plans for the care of your teeth are important. If you brush your teeth twice a day, but your mouth is not clean, even with flossing, then you need to increase your care. Swish water around in your mouth, then brush again. Healthy gums, healthy teeth, good diet, good healthcare. Read the labels on the packages and call or email my office with any questions. More questions?" she asked again.

"No. I just do not want dentures. I looked around a pharmacy store in Shelbyville. I stopped to buy a new toothpaste. The pharmacist was not good with answers. He was this puny guy that was named

Larry. He said that he was supposed to watch for Officer Brewster to pick up the payoff money that the manager had left at the drive through window. Brewster would come by at closing time. That was last night. I was in a shopping blur," he said.

"We have toothpastes samples. I will check the plaque on your teeth. And I will give you some samples with higher concentrations of fluoride to take home," she told him.

Now, she had to decide when to go to Shelbyville, Kentucky to take care of Officer Brewster with the same care that she used to take care of her patients. Bonnie hated drug dealers. And she liked to stop their operating network by getting rid of the payoff cops.

David had a well maintained mouth that required little work. So she cleaned and polished his teeth, then gave him a half priced bill.

He smiled and said, "Thanks for the information."

"Keep coming back. You can help me to learn better ways to contol tooth decay. And please leave comments on my website. Thank you. And have a good evening," she replied.

Bonnie cleaned up part of the office, then she left the rest of the mess for Meredith, her dental assistant. She made some notes about adding information to her website. She needed to add more about fluoride with side effects, root canal therapy, and research on tooth decay. The root canal therapy was a real concern for her. Bonnie thought that it was completely prehistoric to pull a tooth instead of killing an infection.

Killing an infection was like killing a drug dealer to her. It was like wiping out the smallpox virus. She despised dope dealers, thieves, and abusive tyrants. Bonnie was now spending a lot more time getting rid of dope dealers. But, she made sure that her life had a nice balance of fun things, like exercise, and good food, so that she could have a bright side, too.

And she was now going to have to cater to Wally Joe. When she got home, she started cooking another five meals at once. The fried chicken, pork chops, catfish, lasagna, and baked ham, for Wally Joe, would be enough to last for a few more days. She added potatoes and vegetables, and wrapped them up. She wanted Wally Joe happy and out of her way. He was still going to be tired from moving, for at least another week. And that is what she told him when she finally saw him at home.

"Wally Joe, you can just sleep and lounge around with boxes everywhere until you get organized. This is not a hotel. Do what you want to do. Rest, relax, go out, whatever. This is family. And you have all your privacy. I would sleep for two days straight if I had just moved. Then, I would bubble bath the time away for at least another five days," she advised.

He smiled and said, "I was hoping that the two of you would be too busy to notice."

"I am never going to notice anything that you do. I like privacy. And, I respect privacy for others. Carl Silas wants you here. We want you to be happy. You have your own locked space. I have always wanted to have a guesthouse for visitors. I never stay with people in their homes. I always use hotels when I visit. Just be comfortable. You do not have to talk to me each time that you see me. You live here. We live here," Bonnie promised him.

"Carl Silas, must really like you, if he married you," he told her.

"I love my husband. We get along great."

"We have a little friction sometimes. Mostly guy stuff."

"Carl Silas has an idea about what men are supposed to do."

"He likes to believe, what he wants to believe," Wally Joe said.

"I think that he is really open with his opinions."

"That is because he likes smart, good looking women, like you."

"You would be more comfortable with a wife," Bonnie said.

"The both of us, we have always had girlfriends. Never without one, Carl Silas and I."

"So what happened to the girlfriend that you left behind?"

"She did not want to move here. And she was not my wife," Wally Joe told her.

"I hear that from lots of people. This whole state has become a crime infested place full of dope. But, Carl Silas wants to stay here."

"It would be hard to start over, somewhere else," he told Bonnie.

"I want to branch out with more dentist offices in another city."

"I hope you do not branch until I finish medical school. I am already very tense from the lack of stability with being a student again," Wally Joe said.

"We are not going anywhere. Branching, does not mean moving away. You can relax, study, finish medical school. We are not going to sell this house," Bonnie told him.

Wally Joe walked over and hugged her, just as Carl Silas came into the room. And when Wally Joe saw Carl Silas, he would not let go of Bonnie. Bonnie pushed Wally Joe away, so that he would stop holding her. Then Wally Joe released Bonnie. And she turned around and saw her husband. She smiled and said, "Wally Joe thinks that we might sell the house and move. What are we going to do to make him feel safe here?"

"Like I said, Wally Joe the house is always here for you. We will not sell our home. But, that woman is my wife. So watch where you put your hands. Bonnie takes care of everybody in this house. And we have never fought about anything. So, do not cause a fight. She will always help you. She just has to get used to you first. Let her examine and polish your teeth. That is a dentist," Carl Silas said.

Bonnie hugged Carl Silas, and said, "I get to live with two great looking men. Anytime that you want your teeth checked, just asked me, Wally Joe. Your job now is to finish medical school. We can get tickets to ballgames to break up the weekends. I work Saturdays, so you and Carl Silas can have your own good times."

"Fun would help me right now. I am feeling the tension," Wally Joe replied.

"You can stay in your room all the time if you want, Wally Joe. You do not have to go to the games. Just lock the door and act like we are not even here until you finish medical school. You are safe. I bought this place so that I would stay safe. And when you are a physician, you will have lots of money, again. Now, relax and do what you want. We will not knock on your door. Find a wife, and she can stay here, too. I already gave you the car and the money," Carl Silas told him.

"Okay. Then I will call it a night. I may not come out for days," Wally Joe said as he patted Carl Silas on the shoulder and left the room.

Bonnie hugged her husband tightly. Wally Joe had started a little rift between her and her husband that Bonnie wanted to close. Carl Silas hugged her back and said, "If Wally Joe does anything to upset you, just tell me. He does like to roughhouse. And, he probably will get married soon. We did sort of compete a lot when we were kids. But, I can tell that he wants to settle down. He can be married and still go to medical school."

The next morning, Bonnie left early for the office. She stayed another hour after the office had closed, and then headed toward Shelbyville, Kentucky. She parked her car and watched the pharmacy store. A police car went by the drive through window and picked up a bag. Bonnie followed the cop to the pizza restaurant where he parked behind the building. Bonnie parked a few buildings away, near a dumpster.

She walked behind the stores, stood near a dumpster where she could see the police car, and said in a low, deep voice, "Brewster, I am stuck. I have the rest of the payoff money. Help me to get loose."

She saw the police car door open and close. Then Bonnie went the other way so that she could come from behind the cop and away from the police car. She moved quickly and knocked the cop down. A few more hard hits, and Brewster was dead. She ran to her car as she heard some people talking nearby. Taking the side streets and back roads, she meandered back to the interstate and drove toward home.

Bonnie thought about Brewster while she was driving. That was just one payoff cop gone, while there were lots of payoff cops left. She really hated being in this state with the organized crime network. Bonnie just wanted to move away to a place where she could have friends. Her time was spent fighting the mafia and corrupt government officials. She always felt better after she had killed a dope dealer. It was like the air became fresher and some of the stress went away. But, she would like to have a more pleasurable life.

Still, Bonnie would not be able to enjoy herself if she was doing absolutely nothing to stop the drug network. She was feeling the stress and the loneliness of her isolated battle. It was safer to kill the dope dealers her way. And when she was lonely, there was always Carl Silas to be with at home. Her husband had enough money to keep her in a nice house in a safe neighborhood. But she did wonder if her life was really supposed to be a constant battle with the dope gangs that were pushing into more areas.

Driving with great attention to the road, Bonnie finally pulled onto her driveway. Her husband would be home in about another thirty minutes. She raced inside the house and noticed that Wally Joe's car was gone. Wally Joe was going to be a big problem for her if he started noticing when she left and got home. Carl Silas had said that they would probably never even see Wally Joe after he started medical school. Wally Joe would be really tired and busy all the time. She hoped that her husband was right.

After turning on hot bath water and adding grapefruit scented bubble bath, she went to the kitchen to cut up lettuce for a huge salad. Bonnie put the garlic bread in the oven and sliced the vegetables. Carl Silas walked in the door just as she finished pouring the orange juice. He was earlier than usual tonight So she would just soak in the hot bath a little later. She hugged him and told him that she was cold. He said that he was tired and cold, too. So they hugged a little longer before they ate dinner. They ate quietly because they were both worn out from all the preparations for Wally Joe.

Bonnie went to soak for only about an hour in the hot bubble bath before she almost fell asleep that night. She had burned candles in the bathroom with the light turned off. The shadows from the flames had made her feel like she was in a cave. Every muscle in her body had relaxed in the hot water as she had felt herself starting to drift to sleep. Then, she had just stopped soaking and had stumbled to the bedroom.

She woke up at around three o'clock in the morning and decided to read in the guest bedroom because she would probable only run into Wally Joe downstairs. Bonnie settled back on the pale blue comforter as she stretched out on the bed. She liked to read this love story over and over again. Almost memorizing each line, she felt a little happy mood wrap around her.

She liked the stories about knights and noble ladies best. The battles with swords and armor kept her connected with her war on drugs. Bonnie hated dope and dope dealers. Carl Silas was not a knight in shining armor. But, he did keep her safe and warm. He was not ugly. And maybe, he would fight for her on horseback if the circumstances forced the battle. In a lot of ways, Bonnie did not have a very high opinion of her husband. But perhaps, she was just too opinionated. She hated dope and only wanted to fight the dope dealers.

She really did not want to see Carl Silas put to the test. If she was to see her husband to be forced to fight for her, and then, to lose, she would feel worse. And right now, without him ever being forced to fight to protect her, she had to be very careful about what she said to him anyway. So if he were to lose a battle trying to protect her, right in front of her, she might have a problem keeping the sneer out of her voice. More than likely, Bonnie thought that she would be the one to intercede and fight the battle. And Carl Silas really did not need to know how aggressive Bonnie could be in a crisis. That might make him suspect that she was capable of other things quite violent, like murder.

She slowly turned the pages in the book, trying to savor the words. Carl Silas opened the door to the bedroom and smiled. Then he walked over and got under the covers. He put his arm around her and said, "Found you again." Her husband snuggled tightly and closed his eyes.

Bonnie leaned over and kissed his cheek. Then she said, "I just wanted to read awhile. It was so quiet in the house that I did not want to go downstairs and turn on the television."

"Wally Joe is probably down there doing who knows what," her husband said.

"I never really notice him being here. But, he is a guest. And this early in the morning, I may be just a little too relaxed to act completely proper. Besides, now I have my great looking husband holding me while I read. I will not make any noise to keep you awake. Just a few pages turning in a book and the light on."

"You could read in our room," he mumbled slowly.

"I did not want to wake you up."

"I must have got cold. I woke up anyway."

"In a few hours, you will have to get up. Do you want me to turn off the light so that you can sleep?" Bonnie asked him.

"You can read. I just get lonely."

"Just a few more pages," Bonnie told him as she kissed his cheek again. As she read, she watched his face to see if he was going back to sleep. After reading a couple more pages, she noticed that her husband did not go to sleep. He was holding her, but not sleeping. She stroked his dark hair and gently tugged on one of his eyebrows. Carl Silas opened his eyes and watched her.

"You are not sleeping. This is not working out very well. Tomorrow, you are going to be very tired. I am just going to turn off the light. You need your sleep, my little lamb," Bonnie told him.

"Well, only if you want to," her husband replied.

Bonnie listened closely for any sound of victory in his voice as her husband snuggled even closer. She could only hear a muffled voice asking her to keep him warm. So she turned off the light and held him. She was wide awake. But, she could not read anymore if Carl Silas was not going to go to sleep. And she was not going to leave again after he went to sleep. He would probably just wake up and start wandering around the house looking for her.

She wondered if he had nightmares. Carl Silas never talked to her about things like that. Then she thought about Wally Joe being in the house. Because Bonnie spent most of her time working around her husband's moods, she did not always anticipate everything that he might feel. And that could be dangerous for her. Carl Silas might trust her, but he was not a stupid oaf. He was very intelligent. And she did not want him to wonder how she spent her time. She managed to be home when her husband was home.

Maybe he was just a little jealous of the time that she spent with his brother. She did not want him jealous. She wanted him happy and content. But, he was such a selfish person. He had got his way again, because she always let him have control. She was not reading anymore. She wide awake, holding her husband, and waiting for the sun to come up. But, it was him and his money that made her safe and without thieves, each and everyday. So she held him tightly, trying to keep him from being lonely while he was asleep.

While she was keeping her husband safe in her arms, a few truckers were going after some more dope dealers many miles away. The dope dealers were blocking traffic on a road in southern Jefferson County. The truckers did not like to carry the Louisville loads. But, sometimes they would have to take a load to that city. So they would have to try to avoid the slimy Louisville Metro Police and the false charges, while venturing into Louisville.

The dope dealers had two cars blocking the road. And, there were two truckers trying to drive through. In a real city with real cops, people would just call the police to have the cars moved. But you could not in dope dealing, gangster territory. Jefferson County simply had no laws, no rules, and only swindles.

One of the truckers walked up to one of the cars and asked if he could help. The little ragtag, red haired Caucasian boy in the blue car said that the drivers had to wait. The tall, brown haired, Caucasian trucker smiled at him and said, "Oh. So you are a big pick?"

The red haired boy smiled and replied, "I run this pick, right here." Then the boy tapped his index finger three times in a row.

The trucker smiled again and said, "Okay, big pick. I need to talk to my friend in the other truck." Then he walked back to the other trucker and told him that the picks were just blocking the road. There was not any easy way to turn around.

The other trucker looked at him and winked as he said, "We truck, Louisville." Then, he got out of his truck. And they both walked back to the two cars. The other trucker smiled at the two boys in the cars that were parked across the road.

Then the other trucker told the boys, "Hey big picks, we got something for you from our loads. But, we do not want to get fired. I opened it today and took about fifty of these little boxes. Walk over here so we can give a box to the big picks."

The two boys followed the truckers off of the road. When they were out of the light and in the darkness, the two truckers knocked the boys down and stomped on them. One of the truckers took a metal pipe from his pocket and beat both of the boys to death. Then he said with hatred, "Like I said, we truck, Louisville. My boy is about your age. But you are not my boy. You are dirt."

Then, they walked back to their trucks in silence. And one of the truckers hooked a wooden pallet onto the front of his Peterbilt and slowly pushed each car off the road so that the trucks could get through.

That is why nobody wanted to carry a Louisville load. The dope dealers were nothing but trouble for anybody. Truckers were hard working, dedicated people that brought shipments of everything to every city, just like the railway companies. The drug dealers would only steal and tear up things. Those were two young boys, now dead, because the area had put in dope gangs. Those kids were not ever going to play softball or soccer because they were only drug dealers that robbed and terrorized people.

The cops and the state officials let the gangsters run the whole state. And, young boys died like that in the war over dope. Those same boys could have grown up and went to college. But they were forced into dope gangs by the filthy cops and the corrupt state government. And, the truckers did not have any choice because dope dealers were incorrigible. Drug dealers only hurt people and things. Those boys had to die before they could destroy and wipe out more people.

That is why the truckers had to keep areas free of dope control. If the gangs controlled everything, then there would only be terror everywhere. At least when those truckers went home, they would be safe with their families. Their wives and kids would not be attacked because they were pushing the dope gangs back and away from their home towns.

Dope dealers were lying scum that lived like a parasite on society. Nobody could trust a drug dealer. You just had to push them out, kill them, and wipe them out, like a disease. And those two young boys had died so that the truckers could protect their families and not worry about their own kids.

Chapter 5   Old Friends

Bonnie knew that the marathon race was going to be fun for her today. She was all pumped and ready for some athletic good times with a bunch of power pushing competitors. She was stretching and warming up her muscles for the fifteen kilometer race. Winning was not important to her. Being in the race and supporting jogging were the things that she wanted to do. She always felt great after her races. Everyone said that you were supposed to cool off slowly when you would end a race. Bonnie never wanted to do that. She liked to run hard and fast to the very end. Then she would just stop, while her muscles would start to shake.

That feeling was awesome with the endorphins pumping through her body. She would just drop to ground after a run and let her muscles handle the shock of going from heavy physical exertion to complete relaxation. Her muscles could lock up, but they never did. Her muscles would shake a lot, then just stop shaking. Bonnie really liked the rush. She did not like to take the time to cool down like a racehorse. But, she would never recommend that to anybody else because it could be very dangerous to treat your muscles like that.

You could almost compare it to tempering metal by using heat and cold to make the metal harder and more resilient. The blacksmiths would heat the metal with a flame then dip the metal in cold water to change the brittleness, so that swords would not shatter. Even though she would just stop after a race, Bonnie did want her muscles to stay healthy, flexible, and not hard. It could be dangerous to cool down fast with that sudden shock to her muscles. But she liked the feeling of going from the heat of racing with her muscles pumping fast and hard, to the sudden cool of relaxed muscles.

And she was going to do it again today, just like always. Starting out slow in the race, she stayed with the group of runners at the end. As she picked up speed, she moved to the middle pack of runners. While she was holding that same speed, the other runners from the middle began to drift to the end, so she was now with the front group of runners. Being in the front group, she would pace herself with these runners until about the last part of the race. Near the end, all the runners would run hard for the finish line.

With her final push for speed, she raced with the others to the end. Bonnie was in the front group until the end and crossed the finish line as the fifteenth runner. Dropping to the ground, she poured ice cold water all over her, from the bottle that she had grabbed from the runner's table. Her eyes were closed when she felt hands rubbing her down. It was Wally Joe. He was rubbing her muscles and telling her that she should be walking it off.

Being really pumped from the race, she was extremely fired up and wanted him to leave her alone. His hands were everywhere, without her being able to stop his massage. When her muscles stopped shaking a little, she took a few deep breaths and started thinking about what to say to him. After she had poured more of the cold water on her abdomen, she turned to look at him with the words almost out of her mouth. Wally Joe only tried to push the cold water off of her chest and to keep rubbing her down.

She poured more cold water on her throat which he also tried to push off of her neck. So, she poured the cold water on Wally Joe to see what he would do about that.

He stared at her really hard and said, "You are shaking."

"I always shake after a race. I like it."

"You could go into shock."

"I do not usually go into shock after a race. If I went into shock, then I would probably stop running. Probably, not definitely."

"Probably. You would probably and not definitely stop doing something that could kill you?"

"I run because I like it," Bonnie said.

"None of the other runners dropped to the ground."

"I am not them. You have met me before."

"You made it worse with cold water. Your muscles needed to cool down, not freeze," Wally Joe said.

"If you are this much fun in your first year of medical school, you better not watch me at the gym during your third year. I have been running for years in exactly the same way."

"You could die. Has Carl Silas ever watched you race?"

"He probably works when I race."

"I know that he would put a stop to that dangerous move," he said and tried to pick her up to carry her to a bench.

"I am not a cripple. You can watch me race, but try not to interfere. This is how I relax."

"By killing yourself. I want to take your pulse."

"Go ahead. Take my pulse. Check my heart rate. And, if you will look behind you, will see that you have attracted the attention of the race medics. They are headed this way."

Wally Joe saw them coming with the medical equipment. When they got there, he held out his hand for a stethoscope, and said, "I am a doctor. I need to check her heart." One of the nurses handed him a stethoscope. Wally Joe listened to her heart pumping, felt her neck, and put his hand around her wrist. He told the nurses that she was okay and thanked them for letting him borrow the stethoscope.

After the nurses left, Wally Joe began rubbing her legs again. Bonnie let him do it for a few minutes, then asked him to stop. He did not want to stop. Wally Joe looked at her and said, "I almost believe that Carl Silas does not even care anything about you if he lets you endanger yourself like this. That is not a safe thing to do, Bonnie. I could see your muscles shaking. I thought that you were having a seizure. Carl Silas would blame me if anything happened to you."

"I am a dentist, Wally Joe. And a very experienced runner. Not all runners, not all athletes play their sports the same way. You are under a lot of pressure with school. I was under a lot pressure, too, when I went to school. Carl Silas takes great care of me. I am safe, happy, and in love. You need to relax. If you want to help me right now, you can go get me another bottle of water from that table, for me to drink. I paid a fee to run in this race that includes the water on that table for the runners. Okay?"

He went to get the water while Bonnie relaxed. She was feeling a lot more tense after the race than before because Wally Joe had scared her, the nurses were watching them, and she had to keep talking to him. She started drinking the water that he gave her. Then she said, "I am going to finish this bottle of water. Then we should leave. The nurses are still staring at us. Do not try to carry me again? I am really pumped up from the race. I like that part. I would most likely drink two more bottles of water. But, we need to leave because we have attracted too much attention."

"So maybe I ruined this for you. I will get two more bottles of water and walk you to your car. But, if I think that you are in danger, I will carry you and have an ambulance follow me to your car. I am a doctor," he told her.

"I have my own doctor. My husband is a doctor."

"This is the doctor that is here right now. Do you want me to carry you? I will, you know."

"That will just make it worse for me, Wally Joe. I run marathons all the time without really caring about winning. I just want to run with the pack. With the other people that like the same sport that I enjoy."

"So maybe I enjoyed carrying you."

"Do not do it again. I think that we should just leave. If you want to start training as a jogger, that would be fine. But, unless you understand the sport, you should not try to change the runners. I like to drop to the ground after each race."

"Carl Silas has really never watched you race?"

"My husband does not have to watch me. I do not run to win or for trophies. I just like to race. I suppose if I said that each race was a learning experience, you would understand that. I understand the sport. Now, we need to leave with two more bottles of water."

The nurses were still watching them, so Wally Joe decided to put his arm around Bonnie's shoulders. They walked to her car in silence while Bonnie kept drinking the water. He told her to give him the keys so that he could unlock the door. She just gave him the keys and finished drinking the second bottle of water. He opened the car door for her as she got into the car.

She said, "That was polite. But, just a little too caregiving. I come to these marathons by myself all of the time. And Carl Silas would not like for you to keep holding me. So I am not going to encourage it. Thanks for helping. If I ever go into professional sports, I will not ask you to be my trainer. I realize that you were scared. And that you are pre-doctor. And, that you are not my husband. If we are going to have a friendship, we need to talk about boundaries. Like I said, you are not Carl Silas. You are my husband's brother. You could be my friend or not my friend? Either way, I am married and will be polite. See you at home, pre-doctor."

"Okay. Then, we will try for friends," Wally Joe replied and closed her car door.

Bonnie drove straight to her office. She had the luxury of a full bathroom with shower and tub in her dental suite. She had finished her shower when she heard Meredith coming in to start the evening shift. She thought about how she had written the race date on the calendar in the kitchen at home, so that Carl Silas would know where she was when she was running the marathon. She was drying her hair when Meredith said that she had a phone call. Bonnie told Meredith to put the call on hold or to take a message.

Meredith said that Bonnie's brother was on the phone. She asked Meredith to get the name of the person that was on the phone, because her blood went cold with that information. Bonnie never talked to any of her relatives. Meredith told her that Wally Joe was on the phone. Bonnie said, "That is my brother-in-law, Meredith. Tell him to wait a minute."

When she answered the phone, she said politely, "Now what has happened, Wally Joe?"

"I thought that you were coming home."

"I work second shift today, Wally Joe. And, I am fine."

"Then, will you check my teeth?"

"Yes, we can do that today."

"What did you do with all that sweat from the race?"

"I have a shower in my office. Meredith can tell you when to come tonight for an appointment. I need to finish getting dressed before my patient arrives. I will transfer you back to Meredith."

Bonnie thought that she should call Carl Silas because Wally Joe was becoming just a little too intense. But maybe, he was just lonely and was looking for a friend. She did not want to start the habit of checking in with her husband. However, she could just call, say hello, and chat about Wally Joe for a few minutes.

Her husband answered the phone and said, "What happened?"

"Wally Joe came to watch me run this morning, thought that I dying, and carried me to a bench. Now, he is coming in for an appointment about his teeth. I think that he is lonely. And he may have been scared when he watched me race. He wanted me to cool down slowly. I always cool down in a ice bucket. And, I told him that you would not be too happy if he was pawing on me too much. And that I would not encourage it. And that we could be friends or not friends. Either way, I said that I would help him," she told her husband.

"Pawing on you?"

"He started rubbing me down after the race."

"Yeah, that would be Wally Joe," Carl Silas said.

"Can you find him a wife? He is a nice guy in medical school."

"I will see what I can find."

"I have to see a patient in about five minutes. Have to go. Love you," she told him and hung up the phone.

Bonnie had started saying, love you, a lot, since Wally Joe had moved in. She had been happy not to see Wally Joe at home. The more that she saw of him would only make things worse for her. Her life had two separate parts that were both chosen by her. She could not idly watch people tortured by dope dealing thieves. At the same time, she needed to do research and find better ways for the future. She was fighting the war against dope and working as a dentist.

Wally Joe was early for his appointment with her. She went out to greet him and said, "Meredith will make a chart for you with no charges for the visit so that we can keep track of any problems. Without a chart, we would not be able to identify any issues. And, we can take x-rays to look for hidden problems. Okay?"

"Sounds great," Wally Joe said.

In the examination room, Bonnie told him, "I called Carl Silas after you phoned me for this appointment. We think that you are lonely. He promised to find you a wife."

"What kind of woman do you think that he will pick?"

"My husband picked me. And Wally Joe, like I could have already guessed, your teeth and gums are in great shape, just like your brother. I will give you some toothpastes samples to try for better plaque control and whiteness. We are done. See you at home," she told him.

"Should I wait for you to lock up and leave?"

"No. I lock up all the time. And, Carl Silas knows that you might have been pawing on me. So to make peace, I will just see you at home."

"I am not afraid of Carl Silas."

"I want Carl Silas to be happy and not to worry about anything, Wally Joe. I am not afraid of Carl Silas either. I do not want to hurt him," Bonnie said.

At about that same time, many miles away, two truckers went in through the back gate of Little Sodas Trucking in Louisville, Kentucky. They were walking slowly toward the building where they banged on the outside wall. The dispatcher ran out to find out what had fallen and what was making that noise. One of the truckers hit him in the face with a board from a pallet, and kept hitting him until he fell down. They dragged his body to the stack of pallets behind the building and then hid the corpse in the dumpster.

After that, they wrecked every tractor and trailer on the lot. That dispatcher had been a big problem because part of his job was to damage tractors at other companies and to steal loads from the other companies. He was a gangster that was wiping out the other truckers. And, the Little Sodas employees did not even look for him. One of the employees just told the person that had come to pick up the dispatcher, at the end of the shift, that the dispatcher had walked off of the job. Later that night, the dumpster was emptied and that dispatcher's body was taken away with the trash. Nobody looks for a dope dealing gangster.

During all that time, one of the other truckers in that war, Bonnie, the dentist, had been safely working in her office. She had began cleaning up the office as soon as Wally Joe left. After she had finished the paperwork and had added a few more things to her website, it was almost two hours later, before she finally left for home. Craving chocolate ice cream made her stop at the grocery for pecan chocolate chip ice cream. Driving home carefully, she spooned the ice cream into her mouth until almost the whole pint was gone.

Carl Silas was standing in the kitchen with a beautiful woman when Bonnie walked through the back door. The woman was drinking coffee at the kitchen table while Carl Silas was washing dishes in the sink. When she opened the back door, Wally Joe stepped into the kitchen. And everybody turned to stare at her.

Carl Silas said, "Wally Joe seems to think that you could have been hurt today. I have never seen you run in one of your races. You never said that it was important to you for me to watch you. He said that you were shaking like you were having a seizure. Bonnie, do you think that you might hurt yourself? Maybe all this jogging is not such a good thing."

"People jog all the time Carl Silas," Bonnie told him.

"Yes, I know. But do you have to do it in such a way that it scares Wally Joe? He said that he had to carry you."

"I think that he wanted to carry me."

"That is what I thought, too. Despite the fact that I also know, that watching a person shake after a race is a frightening thing to see. So, I went to find Wally Joe a wife. This is Kathy. I told her that my brother was lonely and needed a wife. And, I asked her if she would come by tonight so that I could force him to start dating her before they got married because my brother likes to rub down my wife," Carl Silas said.

Wally Joe piped in, "I agreed to date this beautiful woman to appease my brother's jealousy. He said that he would give me two full weeks before I had to marry Kathy."

"Well, Wally Joe you can stay here as long as you want. But you will be less lonely with Kathy. And if you live here with your wife, you will probably leave my wife alone. I have worked with Kathy for a long time. We both like kids. Kathy has her own home. But, Wally Joe needs to finish medical school and will be safer here. And I have do something about the way that I have dangled my gorgeous wife right in front of his lonely eyes. We are going to keep you occupied with a woman to talk to, Wally Joe," Carl Silas said.

Kathy added, "I think Wally Joe is great. We will be friends. How could I possibly turn down an opportunity with a doctor?"

"Does anyone need food or anything else? I am exhausted and just want to go to sleep," Bonnie offered.

"Wally Joe had already prepared me for that. He actually believes that you are neglected and should be cared for. And, we usually do keep earlier hours during the business week. I just got Kathy to come over tonight so that we could avoid any problems. Wally Joe is good looking, so we will probably not have to pay woman to talk to him. Do you think that we have the issue in hand, Bonnie?" Carl Silas said as he smiled at his wife.

"Seems to be a working situation, Carl Silas," Bonnie told him.

"If I am to have a shotgun wedding, then I demand to know what kind of engagement the two of you had, which did not even have a huge wedding ceremony for the end. How and why, did you ever marry my brother, Bonnie Blake?" Wally Joe ask.

"Ask your brother. We have found you a wife. You and Carl Silas look a lot like each other, Wally Joe. So Kathy might actually stay with you. And, I have permission from my husband to retire for sleep tonight. Nice to meet you, Kathy," Bonnie offered and left to go upstairs.

She started running the hot bath as soon as she got upstairs. Lighting the candles, she turned off the bathroom light, and soaked in the hot bubble bath while she watched the shadows of the flames. Thinking about her day, she wondered at the news stories that she had read which reported Brewster as missing in Shelbyville. Somebody must have taken the body and the payoff money.

Then, Wally Joe had showed up at her race to make her wonder again. Too much attention could create a lot of problems for her. The hot bath actually woke her up. So she soaked and thought about her day, for about three hours. She heard Carl Silas come up the stairs at about two o'clock in the morning. Wally Joe and Carl Silas had probably just had another very serious talk. There had not been any sounds of broken furniture or wrestling, so maybe the conversation was a little more sensitive this time.

He had found Wally Joe a woman to talk with, in a very short time. Carl Silas probably knew lots of good looking women. And none of that made her jealous either. She was hoping that Carl Silas knew a lot more attractive women to keep Wally Joe occupied. There was no guarantee that this very first woman from here, Kathy, would work out for Wally Joe in the long run. But if Wally Joe would just spend some time with a woman, that alone, would make a little more peace between Bonnie and Carl Silas, while Wally Joe was finishing medical school.

So now that Bonnie was sure that Wally Joe had more people to do things with, she concentrated on her office. The next days were really good for cleaning the office because she only had a few appointments. Bonnie was a person that just kept things clean by being organized. She never had any build up with dirt because her office was designed for cleaning. Some people had to move furniture to clean. Bonnie just had to move the dirt and dust away. After she had finished an early day shift, she drove to Elizabethtown, Kentucky. Carl Silas was teaching that night, so she did not have to go home until much later.

Spending so much time with Wally Joe had made her think of her sister Mindy. And that was not because Wally Joe was a loser like Mindy. Carl Silas was just helping Wally Joe as much as he had helped Bonnie. She had been struggling with the mafia takeover that had hurt the trucking company that her uncle had left her when she had met her husband. Her husband had given her the same safe haven that he had given to Wally Joe so that they both could study. Carl Silas had an expensive home with lots of security to keep all of them safe.

Her trucking company was doing better now. She wanted to branch out with more dentist offices that had second shift hours. That was a social change for dentist office hours that Bonnie was pushing for, among her other endeavors. Right now, she wanted to find out where trouble making Mindy was, without Mindy knowing that she was looking for her. Mindy was dope dealing slime that had probably already ruined lots of families.

Bonnie worked her way toward Shepherdsville from Elizabethtown and stopped for gas. Some of the drug dealers that were parked outside the store were talking about Mark Tyler. That Louisville Metro Police Officer had come to Bullitt County to try to collect more drug payoff money. She had went to the same high school as Tyler. Mark was slime that she had seen collect drug money before.

They said that Tyler was in Iroquois Park in Louisville tonight. So Bonnie took the side streets and back roads to get near the park. At six o'clock in the evening, the park was deserted. She watched for the Louisville Metro Police Officer. Then she spotted Tyler.

He was pompously walking through the park. Bonnie could see the tiny dead children in her mind that were being destroyed because of his drug traffic with nefarious butchers. She had jogged to the top of that hill many times in the past. Usually, she would get a banana split at the ice cream shop that had been across the street after her run. Now, she was glad that the ice cream parlor had closed, because she wanted everything in Louisville to be closed.

She parked her car behind an insurance office building that was a few blocks away from the park. Then, she slowly walked to the park and stayed behind the trees to watch for Tyler. He was walking down the path. Bonnie stepped behind Mark when he passed her and slammed his head against the pavement. He was unconscious, bleeding, and freezing. She used her strength to make sure that he was dead in the next few seconds. She thought to herself, imagine that, a payoff officer killed in Louisville, Kentucky. And she also knew that there must be hundreds more of those lousy cops left in the city.

She walked back to her car and slipped out of Louisville without attracting any attention. Bonnie had that same feeling of peace and cleansing that she had experienced each time that the other disgusting drug dealers had died. First, she would have this absolutely livid surge when she spotted a dope dealer. Then, she would carry that hate with her as she would kill that dope dealer because they had terrorized her and others.

As she was driving back through Shepherdsville, she thought that she saw Beth Hempson stop at a store. Bonnie drove to the store across the street so that she could watch and see what happened. The driver looked like Beth, but was not Beth. Then, something popped up in the back seat. There was a person back there that had sat up and also looked like Beth. The driver came back to the car and tossed a drink to the back seat.

Bonnie recognized Beth as she sat up and opened the drink. The driver turned around and said something to Beth. Then, Beth slumped down across the back seat of the car. Bonnie decided to just follow for a little while, as long as things stayed safe for her. The car stopped ahead on the road and pulled off to the side. After a few minutes, the driver dragged Beth out of the back door onto the side of the road, and then drove off. Bonnie passed the spot, and turned her car around, deciding to walk to Beth. Wearing gloves, she walked up to Beth and asked her what had happened.

Beth just stared at her, then she opened her eyes really wide. Beth looked stoned on dope. She licked her lips and said, "Bonnie. Bonnie is that you? I did not do it. I tell you that I really mean it. They set me up."

"Who set you up?" Bonnie asked.

"They did. I told them that I did not do it."

"Beth you have always done it. And, you have always lied about doing it."

"Not this time. This time, they set me up. I just know that I did not do it."

Bonnie kneeled closer to her, in the bushes along the side of the road, where the driver had dragged her, and said, "Who tied you up?"

"I knew it. I just knew it. I can not move. I am tied up. Where are we, Bonnie? How did we get here?"

"You drove here, Beth. Then, you crawled into the bushes. You are high on dope. You are not tied up. You are just stoned out of your mind and can not move."

"I knew it. I just knew it. How did I get stoned, Bonnie?"

"Have you seen Mindy lately?"

"Did she tie me up?"

"You are not tied up. You just will not move. What about Mindy? Have you seen Mindy?"

"She is running big dope out here, Bonnie. Her gang went after my dope gang. We hit her gang a couple of times. I told Mindy that we got her. I knew that we got her. I just knew it. Some of her people are dead."

"Did you help kill them, Beth?"

"You know, Bonnie, I think that they tied me up after I killed them. I can not move. I know that I can not move. I just know it."

"Do you go to dope meets, Beth?"

"I have to. They said that I joined. I knew that I had to go. I just knew it."

"Where did you break in, Beth?" Bonnie softly asked her. She had avoided Beth for years because she was a trashy, trouble making person.

Beth said, "We stole some stuff, Bonnie. I just knew that I had to steal some stuff. I just knew that I had to. How do I get out of here?"

"You know what, I saw your Dad a few months ago. He asked me out on a date."

"Page will explode if she knows about that. She is running dope, too. Page likes to hit. James will not like it when she hits him, again. Page tried to kill him for the life insurance policy and he moved out."

"So you like being a pick, running dope, breaking in houses?"

"Yeah. Pick is great. I have to. I just know that I have to. I do not have a job. I like those little blue pills the best."

"I think that there is a problem here. Look that way, Beth. I think that your hair is caught on something," Bonnie told her. And Beth turned her head, which gave Bonnie a good opportunity to hit Beth with the metal pipe that Bonnie had in her jacket pocket. Beth's hat caught all the blood while Bonnie pounded her head harder. Beth was dead when Bonnie walked back to her car. And, Mindy was running dope somewhere in this city.

Bonnie drove home without stopping anywhere, so that she would be there when Carl Silas got home tonight. She hurried with the catfish for supper so that she could get into a hot bubble bath for a little while. So supper was cooking in the oven and she was soaking in a hot bubble bath, when she heard him open the back door as he came into the house. Walking to the top of the stairs, she told him that she was going to put on some sweats and come down. He went into the kitchen to look over dinner.

While they were eating, he asked, "So, how are things between you and Wally Joe? Any problems?"

"I have not seen Wally Joe for a few days. He does not have any friends here. And he is not a kid. You gave him some people to talk with. Maybe he thought that he would just hang out with your friends for awhile. I am trying to make my first million, so that we can be super rich and live the good life while we are still young. Now, might be a good time for us to join a few country clubs. Wally Joe could go and meet some wealthier people, while we were making some more business contacts."

"Country clubs? They do not bring country clubs to you. You have to go there," Carl Silas said with a little dismay.

"And everybody else gets into the hot tubs. And I know that you do not want to go to a country club. I just think that Wally Joe is lonely. He did not move here with a wife and kids," Bonnie said softly.

"He has an apartment here that is very private. After he finishes the first year of medical school, he will be adjusted to the change. Then just a few more years, and he will be gone again. I got married because I was lonely, too. Just tell me about any problems with him, so that I can take care of them for you," Carl Silas promised her.

They both went right to sleep that night. The night was quiet with the sounds of only slumber, until Bonnie woke up at about four o'clock in the morning, and could not go back to sleep. She was awake and at the same time, too tired to work on anything. Stretching for a little while, she finally gave up, and came downstairs to watch television.

Wally Joe was in the kitchen looking for something when she came downstairs. Bonnie just dropped onto the couch and started watching a love story. When Wally Joe heard the television, he came to see what was happening. He looked at Bonnie and said, "Did I wake you up? I was looking for a tea strainer."

"There are about four of those in the second drawer on the left side of the sink," she told him.

"Which one of those can I use?"

"They are all the same. I bought this tea that had a strainer in each package. In fact, there are two boxes of that chamomile tea in the top kitchen cabinet. You can have one of those boxes, if you want. And, you will find a tea strainer inside. I was about to make a cup of something, anyway."

"Do you have to go in early today?"

"No. Meredith schedules the appointments as close together as possible, so that sometimes I get a free day. She will be at the office and will call me if there is an emergency."

"Free day. Very nice. Now you can rest."

"Resting will not make me a millionaire. I want to have Sunday office hours. But that day is really the one day, that Carl Silas and I use to do things. I am going to clean up the house today."

"Want to make some tea?" Wally Joe asked.

"Yes, I do. Carl Silas thinks that you are lonely. The apartment was for study and privacy, because he knows that medical school does not allow much time for socializing. And, adults do not really hang out like kids. The whole idea about this house is that it is safe. We do not want big groups coming in and out. Most houses in this state are burglarized every day. We talked about joining a country club, so that you could make wealthier friends. What do you think?" Bonnie asked him.

"I think that most of my time will be spent studying."

"Try calling your old friends. I know that once you move, people usually do not really care anymore about keeping contact with you. You just need to have some new friends. And, Kathy is good for conversation," Bonnie told Wally Joe.

They went into the kitchen and made some hot tea. Bonnie got some things out of the cabinets, so that she would be ready for cooking breakfast. There was about two hours left for watching television before she would have to start making breakfast for Carl Silas. So they drank hot tea, and watched the love story which made Wally Joe even lonelier. Bonnie was so cozy that she was ready to go back to sleep when Carl Silas got up.

Her husband came downstairs to look for her. He found her curled up on the couch while his brother was stretched out in a chair with the ottoman. Walking behind his wife, he wrapped his arms around her shoulders. Bonnie did not even move when he touched her. So he leaned over and looked at her face, noticing that her eyes were closed. His wife was softly asleep among the sofa pillows.

Carl Silas sat on the sofa and held her in his arms until she woke up. Bonnie sagged into his hold and tried to get warmer. That was exactly wanted he wanted her to do. They sat like that for about twenty minutes, before she ask about the time. Her husband told her that they could probably have breakfast in about thirty more minutes. She had already gotten the food out of the refrigerator. She just needed to cook it.

Bonnie was wearing one of his T-shirts with her sweats. Her hair was pulled back behind her head into a twisted knot with a hair barrette. She cuddled closer into his hold for more warmth because she was always cold. Her eyes were only open enough for her to see what was happening.

Bonnie relaxed for a few more minutes, before she ask, "When do you want me to start cooking breakfast? Meredith was able to keep the appointments free for me today. So, I thought that I would clean the house and do some laundry. Do you need something?"

"What I need is to sit right here, just like this. Twenty more minutes and we can start cooking. Right now, I just want to look at my beautiful wife in her favorite colors of lilac, yellow, and white," her husband told her.

Wally Joe said, "Bonnie said that you might join a country club. I am deep enough into medical school to know that I am going to spend most of my time studying."

"When I went to medical school, I lived with Mom and Dad. I was not lonely. My friends were right there. And Mom and Dad only wanted to help me. You will need to do something to break up the monotony. And to keep from becoming too attached to my wife," Carl Silas said.

Bonnie moved just a little and added, "You could try online dating services or chats for those times at three o'clock in the morning when you want to talk to someone. Maybe you could just marry Kathy so that you could have a wife while you are in medical school."

"I probably do take marriage a little more seriously than just to marry Kathy for a little while, like buying a pet so that I would not be lonely for a few years. I will need to be serious if I pick a wife. Do you still see any of your friends from school, Bonnie?" Wally Joe asked.

"No. I moved," she told him. Bonnie did not add that she did not like her friends. In fact, she hated her friends enough to kill them, just like Beth. Instead, she went into the kitchen and started cooking breakfast for them. Carl Silas watched her while he was drinking his orange juice. He was slicing his toast and looking at her at the same time. When she brought him his eggs, he pulled her onto his lap and held here there. She leaned back to stare into his eyes, to try to guess what he was going to do or to say next.

What Carl Silas did do was to hold her tighter and say, "The house does not have to be cleaned today. I have plenty of clean clothes. If you are tired, why not just go back to sleep? My brother thought that you were dying because you pushed yourself so hard in that marathon. Take a day off to relax."

"Okay. I will go back to sleep when you leave. When I wake up, I will take a bubble bath until I am tired of the water. With the time that is left, I will do what I can about the house and laundry. Your dinner will be ready on time."

"I do know how to cook. I just like your cooking better than mine. Now, Wally Joe and I have to leave in about ten more minutes. And you will have your time alone," Carl Silas said.

After they left the house, she went to sleep. Bonnie woke up at three o'clock in the afternoon. She put a turkey in the oven and went to run a hot bubble bath. Only soaking for about two hours in the hot bath, left enough time for her to dust and vacuum the carpet while the laundry was drying. Then she jogged in the kitchen and went to empty the washer and the dryer between each load of laundry.

She thought about Beth Hempson and wondered how many people she had ruined. Somebody had hated Beth enough to leave her for dead along a roadway. Beth had been so high on dope that she did not even know what was going on. She could not even fight the person that had dragged her out of the car. Beth was just a slimy loser that wasted everybody's time.

Bonnie did not know if Page and James would be upset or relieved about Beth's death. If they knew about how Beth was terrorizing everybody, then they might be relieved. If they were under the impression that their daughter was a nice person, then they might be upset. However, you would have to be blind to think that Beth was a nice person. She was a selfish, dope dealing, conniving rat that swindled and robbed people.

While she was hoping that nobody would try to contact her for Beth's funeral, Bonnie put out some fresh potpourri and lit some candles to freshen the house. She did not want people to be looking for her so that she would go to funerals. They might call her office. In fact, if Beth's body was found, then James Hempson might even use that as an excuse to call her. But, there were plenty of excuses for Bonnie to use so that she could stay away from any and all funerals.

The most likely thing to happen, was that Beth's body would not be found unless a road crew went through the area. Because somebody had left her there to die, probably not one person would be looking for Beth. She was like Mindy. She was a person that people would want to avoid, and that only made problems. Maybe the person that had left Beth for dead, would come to pick up the body.

Bonnie went to make the dumplings for Carl Silas to have with his turkey. She made half of the dumplings with added spinach because Bonnie really liked spinach in everything. She was happy while she was cooking, knowing that Beth was not going to be able to destroy any other lives. Beth was dead like all dope dealers should be if there was any justice at all. And, Bonnie always wanted to part of the justice that killed dope dealers.

She made a pumpkin and a cherry pie. Then, she added cranberries and sweet potatoes to the dinner. Bonnie was taking the fresh baked bread out of the oven when her husband came in the back door. He smiled at the large feast that she had prepared on her day off. She was just standing there, looking gorgeous as usual. So he decided to stare at her for awhile longer.

Carl Silas wondered in awe at the way that he had somehow managed to get this woman to become his wife. She was smart, beautiful, efficient, and fun to have around. She took care of everything with complete ease. Bonnie was organized without being a workaholic. She also liked to relax and take those bubble baths of hers for hours and hours. And, his wife was always polished looking. She never looked like an over used work horse. She was as beautiful as any supermodel.

Bonnie started watching her husband as he stared at her. She wondered if there was a problem. Maybe there was something wrong with Wally Joe. She thought that maybe Carl Silas had noticed something that was out of place about how she spent her time. So she walked over to Carl Silas and hugged him, while she tried to soften him up a little. Then she said, "The turkey is done. Everything is ready. I just added a few extras that I wanted, to your turkey dinner."

"Did you sleep today?" he asked her.

That was a normal question for him to ask her. So she thought that perhaps everything was still alright between them and that he was not curious about anything that she done. Wally Joe could be watching her more closely than her husband ever had. And she had spent her entire off day at home so that she could encourage his trust a little more. She looked into his eyes, and said, "Yes. I went to sleep this morning, after you left. And, then I had time to straighten up the house and do some other things."

"I am glad. But, that probably means that you will wander around tonight. You see, I am used to you. And, I do miss you when you are not there, even when I am sleeping," he told her.

"I could go to sleep right now. And, you know that I never want to keep you awake. There have been just a few nights, lately, when I have not slept through the entire night."

"Wally Joe has never said anything about that. So, I guess that he has not noticed."

"I will never go downstairs anymore when I wake up in the middle of the night. I will just take a hot bath and watch the little television in the bathroom. The extra cord for the cable T.V. service is long enough to reach the other bathroom. And besides, Wally Joe is worried about his career, not about me. We make him safe here. Just like you make me safe here," she told Carl Silas.

"So, you are feeling safe and just not sleeping. Are you happy here, Bonnie?"

"I am always happy with you. I love to be with you. Now we should eat or we will have to warm up the food again," she told him as she smiled.

So Carl Silas was only worried about her not sleeping. Bonnie was always waiting for the day when he might say something else that may be about her murders. That could be a difficult conversation. But for now, all that she had to worry about was his concern for her insomnia. She would solve that by pampering him more and by encouraging him to do more physical things to wear him out. Then, he should be very tired and sleep soundly. And hopefully, he would not miss her at night when she could not sleep.

She did not want to just stay in bed because he might wake up if she was gone. So, he was used to her being there, with him. They would work that problem out. And, if he did wake up, he was old enough to find her if he wanted to find her. So she would just try to tire him out with activities so that he would not wake up so easily. And, she was going to keep two more blankets on the bed so that he would stay warm, with or without her.

However, tonight was a problem for her because she had slept during most of the morning hours. So Carl Silas was very tired after supper while she was not very tired at all. When they went to bed, Bonnie slept for a few hours. But she was wide awake again at two o'clock in the morning. She made sure that he was under all the covers. Then, she slid to top of the white comforter that was on the bed, and stretched out. Bonnie picked up her book with the tiny reading light clipped to the pages.

She propped up a pillow so that she could block any light that might shine on Carl Silas, and started reading her book. Being too hot and restless, she did not want to stay under covers. But she was near enough to her husband so that she could notice if he was awake. And Carl Silas was staying asleep. She was doing fine for about for about an hour. Then, Bonnie wanted some more turkey to nibble on.

She went downstairs to the kitchen, walking quietly through the house. While she was putting everything on a plate, Wally Joe came into the kitchen. He was looking at her very closely. So Bonnie stopped and watched him. She was only wearing one of her husband's old T-shirts. But his shirts were long enough to be dresses on her. Then she smiled, and said, "We have lots of turkey, Wally Joe. Want to fix a plate for yourself?"

"Turkey. You cooked a whole turkey. Just like Thanksgiving," Wally Joe said with admiration.

"Turkeys are easy. They cook for a long time so that you can do something else."

"People always complain about all the work that they have to do to cook a Thanksgiving dinner."

"They just need to be organized. If they would cook that same meal many more times during the year, then they would be faster. Fried chicken can take a long too, until you get used to cooking it. I cook turkeys all the time because my husbands like them," Bonnie told him.

"Carl Silas said that about you. He said that you were very organized. And, that you could do anything."

"Just takes getting used to doing something. Like playing any sport."

Wally Joe got a plate and piled up a big stack of food for himself. The turkey was almost gone now. He smiled at her and said, "Thanks for the holiday. I needed a little celebration right now. I am worn out from studying." Then he leaned forward and kissed her lips.

Bonnie stepped back and stared at him. She thought for a long moment before she said, "That is just turkey, Wally Joe. You can always eat what you find in our refrigerator. But you really do not need to kiss me just because I gave you a nice meal when you were so wiped out. Carl Silas would not like that. And I am married to your brother, so you should not kiss me, not even just a little playfully."

"That kiss did not hurt you. I am starving," Wally Joe told her.

"I just asked you not to do that again."

"I am not afraid of Carl Silas. I never ask him if I can do anything."

"I love Carl Silas. And, I am not afraid of you, either."

Then Carl Silas laughed out loud as he stood in the kitchen door. He smiled at Bonnie and said, "So everybody came to get some more of that turkey that I was dreaming about."

"I did not mean to wake you up again by being gone. In fact, I would have already been back if I had not run into Wally Joe. I have a tiny reading light for my book. And, I watched you for over an hour, to make sure that just a little light would not wake you up. Then, I wanted a snack," she told her husband.

"I will always miss you when you are gone, Bonnie. And I just watched my brother kiss my wife, after she fed him. Wally Joe, I warned you about kissing my wife," Carl Silas said.

Wally Joe picked up one more slice of turkey and said, "I am starving. And, you know that I always tip with a great meal. I just did not have any change with me, so I kissed her for a tip."

"You kissed her with the first chance that you got. That was the way that I saw it. You have always been a smooth talker. And, Wally Joe, you can eat my food. But, I will not share my wife with you. And, I was hoping to have some turkey for myself. Do you suppose that you are going to leave any?" Carl Silas complained.

Wally Joe picked up another slice of turkey and said, "I think that you are just about out of turkey, Carl Silas."

"I see a slice right there," he told Wally Joe. And he grabbed a slice of turkey from Wally Joe's plate and ate it. Then he reached to grab another slice from Wally Joe's plate. Wally Joe moved his plate away from Carl Silas. But, Carl Silas moved even closer so that he could take some more turkey from Wally Joe's plate.

"I give up. Unless I leave this room right now, all my food will be gone. I have already said that I am starving," Wally Joe announced as he moved to leave the kitchen.

"And, keep your hands off of my wife. I knew that she would push you away. Be glad that she only told you not to kiss her again. She could have done something much worse, Wally Joe. And remember that we have a game in the morning. So pack any food that you want before we leave. Bonnie is not going to pack lunches for us," Carl Silas said while he laughed.

"I could pack lunches for you. How did your mother ever handle you and Wally Joe?" she asked her husband.

"We were never really home at the same time. Mom did what she could. But, Wally Joe is just not used to me being married. He did have a habit of trying to steal kisses from girls when he could. I just thought that he was flirt. But, he really should not kiss you. And, you did make that point very clear with him. I think that people really just need to tell him no, so that he will stop doing something that they do not like. So I told him no, again. And, Wally Joe does like to pick a fight on occasion, because he thinks that it is funny to argue."

"You are a lot more serious than your brother, even if the two of you do look so much alike," Bonnie said.

"Well, I am more serious around you. Honestly, we both used to act a little unconventional because we are both spoiled. And, my mom still thought that I was acting wild when I married you so quickly. Remember we did not even date. It was just love at first sight. And I did not want to waste any time, so we just got married. That was very unconventional."

She hugged her husband. Then they sat at the kitchen table and ate the late night snack. Carl Silas really did not seem to be concerned about Wally Joe. And, Bonnie had no idea how they had each acted around the other one's girlfriend, because she had not been there. Maybe Carl Silas was more like his brother than she thought. But, she had only known that Carl Silas was very serious and that he did not like to be alone.

And that was part of the problem. Wally Joe was like his brother and did not like to be alone either. But in their house, Wally Joe was alone. Bonnie and Carl Silas had each other. And Wally Joe, he was just by himself, like an only child.

That is why a kid without a brother or a sister is so lonely. That kid watches television alone, plays in the yard alone, and does not have another kid to talk with, that lives in the same house. But, there are two parents who can talk to each other. So the child gets lonely without another child for companionship. That was not exactly the way that Wally Joe felt. But, that was sort of close.

Chapter 6   Few Connections

Bonnie really wanted to be a millionaire, with all of the luxuries, so that she would have lots of money to fight organized crime Then when she was a millionaire , if she did not like a corrupt business, she could start up her own competitive company and push out the bad business. Doing things like that would help improve the business market. And, she would also have to cater to Carl Silas, and not let him feel neglected or lonely, while she working hard to become super rich. She believed that money was power.

So, they joined a few country clubs to help them make more business contacts. Carl Silas liked to play golf at the private clubs with Wally Joe. The two of them were both acting like doctors promoting a private practice. As a C.P.A., Wally Joe had worked for a company that had provided exclusive membership at a private club for the accountants. He had played a lot of golf with his co-workers and friends. When had he moved in with them, he had never mentioned that he liked to play golf.

Carl Silas knew that his brother liked to play golf and had noticed that Wally Joe did not bring his golf clubs with him. To make things simple, they bought two sets of golf clubs when they joined the country clubs. Bonnie would be able to use any of the clubs if she played. However, she had never learned to play golf and thought that she might just take a few lessons to learn the game in the future. So for right now, Carl Silas and Wally Joe could play golf with the two sets of golf club while she could just hang out around the club to check out the members.

She just wanted to take a few lessons, just enough to learn golf without annoying her husband. So that when they played together, she would then know the basics and could have fun with her husband while she was improving with her game. She knew that even though he might be willing to teach their kids some things, he could become irritated if he had to teach her to play golf. Teaching her would slow down his game. Bonnie was always careful to avoid any problems with Carl Silas. She only wanted him to be happy and spoiled.

That was part of the reason that she had been so surprised when Wally Joe had come to her marathon race. He had thought that her husband probably went to watch her run all the time. The fact that Carl Silas was not there, made it look like they might have a problem with their marriage. Bonnie really wanted her marathon races to be her time that was spent alone. She did not have to cater to Carl Silas while she was running in a race. All that she had to do was blend in with the other runners and push herself hard. She doubted that Carl Silas would have panicked like Wally Joe, if her husband had seen her shaking after the race.

It might have been nice to have a husband that would take care of her all the time. That kind of husband would let her relax and not make her nervous. She always considered Carl Silas to be just another job that she had to do. They talked about things, planned for the future, and discussed how they would bring up their kids. Yet, he was just another task that Bonnie had to take care of, something that she had to do. Since Wally Joe had moved in, her husband had become publicly expressive of his affection for her. She thought that he was mostly trying to keep Wally Joe off of her by showing him that they had a great marriage.

Bonnie really did not want Carl Silas to pay much attention to anything that she did. She had lulled him into a spoiled life with a beautiful wife that could use her free time to do what she wanted to do. She really wanted him to be happy so that he would not bother her. Wally Joe had sort of challenged that set up because he was expecting more of an intimate relationship between her and her husband.

Playing golf would help all three of them. Bonnie could make business contacts and find new patients. Carl Silas could play at his leisure and spend more time with his brother. And Wally Joe, who was good at playing golf, could find new friends, and find new business associates. She had been pleased with the way that Carl Silas had liked the country clubs and golf courses. And she had told Wally Joe to just put a set of the new golf clubs with his other personal things so that he could play when he wanted. She could just use the clubs that Carl Silas liked for himself, when she took her golf lessons because she only wanted to learn the game and not turn into a golf pro.

While Carl Silas and Wally Joe were away playing golf, she decided to clean out around the gutters and the garage. Bonnie looked for clogged drainpipes by going up and down the ladder all around the house. She rummaged through the garage, looking for a long handle or hose to push through the drainpipes. When she found the older, slightly cracked garden hose, she went back outside and pushed the hose through every drainpipe. When she was putting the garden hose back in the garage, she saw a brown golf bag behind some wooden boards. There were five golf clubs in the torn golf bag. She cleaned up the golf bag and clubs.

When Carl Silas got home, she asked him, "Whose golf bag is in the garage? I found an older bag with five clubs and cleaned it up."

"That is why I bought new golf clubs. That bag is too old and worn out. I was going to throw it away with those battered clubs that I had stored in the garage loft," he told her.

"If you were going to throw it away, then can I use it with those clubs for my lessons? I do not really like to play sports that require so much equipment. You have your set of clubs. Wally Joe has the other set to use. And, right now, I just want to learn the game of golf. If I want a set of new golf clubs, then I can buy some later. The golf clubs and bag were going to be trash anyway."

"Those clubs will be good enough for you to learn the game. And, I can use my new golf clubs at anytime, because you will not need to borrow them for lessons. I noticed that you had the ladder against the house."

"I cleaned out the gutters and drainpipes," Bonnie told her husband.

Wally Joe just stared at her and said, "You cleaned out the gutters. You climbed up on the roof while your husband was playing golf." "I did not use the golf clubs to clean out the gutters. I ran an older water hose down the drainpipes to loosen the debris," Bonnie told Wally Joe.

Carl Silas smiled at Wally Joe and said, "Her muscles are not shaking. Do you think that we should still carry her somewhere so that she can sit down? Like I told you, Wally Joe, she does what she wants to do."

While Bonnie was safely sleeping at home that night, about twenty truckers went into Tagal Trucking in Louisville, Kentucky. Two of the truckers shoved the dope dealing dispatcher into an office closet. Then they got the keys to the tractors that were on the lot and crashed all the tractors into the maintenance building on the property. Then those two truckers went back inside to get the dispatcher out of the office closet because he could identify them. One of them smashed his skull, before they both rolled him up in some tarps and threw him in the dumpster.

Then that same group of truckers walked to the next trucking company that was about a block away and did the same thing. Then they went to one more trucking company that was within walking distance to do the same thing. The dispatch at the third business was locked in and did not wanting to open the door. One of the truck drivers told him that it was an emergency and that he needed to use the phone. The dispatcher still would not open the door. The trucker was watching the dispatcher through the window as he asked him to just hand out the phone through the window opening.

When the dispatcher was handing the phone to the trucker, one of the other truckers grabbed the dispatcher's wrist and broke it. Then the truckers slammed through the window and went into the building. The dispatcher said, "You stay away from me," as he started to run away.

One of the truckers that was named Mike, whispered, "We do not want to stay away from you. That is why we came in here. We want the keys to the tractors. Give me the keys and you do not get hurt."

"I was already hurt!" the dispatcher yelled back at him.

Mike whispered again, "Then you will not get hurt again like this, if you give us the keys." And then he slammed the dispatcher's head with a stapler.

"You are lying! You just hurt me again, " the dispatcher whined.

"No. That is a promise. I will not do this again if you give us the keys," Mike whispered as he hit the dispatcher in the face with the stapler. Then, he hit the dispatcher in the face again with the stapler.

"Stop it!" the dispatcher whined.

Mike whispered again, "I stop this when I have the keys." And, he just kept hitting the dispatcher in the face with the stapler.

"The keys are on that yellow board," the dispatcher told them.

"Now I stop this, " Mike whispered as he stopped hitting him with the stapler. Then, he hit the dispatcher in the face with a board from a pallet.

The other truckers grabbed the keys and wrecked the tractors on the lot, while Mike finished killing the dispatcher and threw him in the dumpster. The truckers hated the Louisville gangsters and wanted to push the Louisville trucking companies out of business. The Louisville dispatchers and truck drivers hit the other trucking companies all the time by destroying and stealing their loads.

The next morning, Bonnie got a phone call from Leo, one of her Lotus Trucking drivers. Leo told her that some of the Louisville trucking companies had been hit really hard at their companies. He said that all the tractors had been wrecked on their properties.

Bonnie said, "Thanks for the call. I will phone our clients and send emails to tell them that we heard about the Louisville problem. I will reassure them that we will protect their loads and our drivers."

"We always protect our loads. And Bonnie, we need some more people to drive team. All of our tractors have the two privacy sleeping compartments, so nobody is afraid to go to sleep anymore, when they drive team. When are you going to drive team with me? With those new compartments that you had installed in the sleepers, not even your husband would mind if you drove team with me, " Leo ask.

She smiled and told him, "I am packed and ready to go. I like those privacy compartments, too. But, now I have an office job and have to stay here. I am still trying to build up more business for us. What else happened? You need to protect yourself on the road. And, I have subscribed to that daily capsule news for the truck satellites, so that you can watch the news and keep up on events while you are on the road. Now I am going to hand out razors so that all my truckers can shave their armpits. If you do not have sleeves, then you better look smooth. Lots of the professional athletes do that anyway. You need to look presentable for the customers. Thanks for calling, Leo. That is how you can protect your job. By keeping me informed."

"Probably that is all that happened. I need to get going to. See you on the road, Bonnie. We truck, Louisville," Leo said and hung up.

When she turned around, Wally Joe was standing right behind her. He ask her, "Is Leo the guy from the country club?"

Bonnie felt her temper rising. Wally Joe appeared to be very close to eavesdropping on her conversation. She wondered if Wally Joe was watching her too closely. Taking a few deep breaths, she looked at him as he stood in her office at home, while she was pretending to write something down.

"Leo is a truck driver, Wally Joe. Do you need something?" Bonnie said.

"Yes. I need to know if Carl Silas is going to be late tonight. I never call him at the office. But, I do want to talk to him," Wally Joe told her.

Bonnie picked up the phone and called her husband. Bonnie told her husband, "Wally Joe wants to talk to you and did not want to bother you at the office. I am going to give him the phone and walk out of the room. He probably did not understand that we do call each other a lot." She handed Wally Joe the phone and left the room.

When Wally Joe came out of her office, she told him, "Wally Joe, everything in the house is yours to use like Carl Silas told you. But, I have decided to start locking my home office room. There are things in there that are personal to other people. I always lock my patient files in a cabinet. And even if you are my brother-in-law, people may tell me things that they do not want to tell you. It is not an insult. I am just giving respect to the privacy of other people. Okay?"

"Okay," Wally Joe said.

"If you need something, just ask. I would not want just anybody to be able to go through personal files. Now, I have to go," she told him.

Wally Joe was reminding her more and more of Beth and Mindy. Mindy was always so sneaky. Maybe Wally Joe needed to have more distractions. He was just supposed to finish medical school and leave, not watch her. She thought about how Beth had once thrown a pair of surfer sandals out onto her parents backyard, for the dogs to chew up, after Bonnie had given her the sandals. Beth had whined for things and then just threw them away.

When Bonnie got to the office, Meredith told her that Wally Joe had called to ask if she had arrived safely. That made Bonnie very angry. She did not have to check in with her husband and, most certainly, was not going to start checking in with Wally Joe. So she called Carl Silas again, and said, "Now Wally Joe has called Meredith to find out if I was at the office. I told him that I was going to start locking my home office room at the house out of respect for the privacy of others. We have never had any problems like that. But, with Wally Joe and Kathy, I should respect and protect the personal information that is in that room."

"Lock the office if you want to. Maybe he just called to ask you something. Why not just call him? He just wanted to ask me something about school. Got to go. Anything else?" Carl Silas asked her.

"No. I will call him. Love you, " Bonnie said as she hung up.

She called Wally Joe and said, "Meredith said that you had called. Need something? Did I give you my personal phone number or not?"

"I did not want to call your personal phone."

"Wally Joe, my husband and I call each other all the time. That is how we see each other during the day. You can always call my personal phone, anytime, day or night, just to chat. I am not that formal."

"I wanted to play golf with Kathy. But, she does not have any golf clubs. I just wondered if she could borrow your golf clubs."

"My golf clubs are salvaged from the trash. Why not use the other set of golf clubs that Carl Silas liked?"

"We could also rent some golf clubs. Kathy can not play golf. I was going to teach her. I think that she might just dig some pretty deep holes with her swings and ruin the new set. I did not even ask Carl Silas. I needed to find some junky golf clubs," Wally Joe said.

"The golf clubs are in the garage, in a brown golf bag behind the water hose. They are my starter set to learn with. Kathy will probably not break all the clubs. Besides, I think that the metal will just bend. Take the golf clubs. Then, Kathy might teach me to play. Go to go. I have a patient," Bonnie told him and hung up.

When she left the office, she drove to eastern Kentucky, and looked over some places that might be good for a truck stop. Lotus Trucking needed to expand operations with more business. And Bonnie wanted to have truck stops with hot tubs for the drivers. After driving on the road as a trucker, she knew lots of the problems that the drivers had to needlessly deal with simply because nobody really cared enough to change things. Being able to make improvements and to offer better services, was why she wanted to be rich enough to have the power to influence businesses.

She had her own truckers to carry the loads, so the most that might happen would be loss of power or water at a truck stop. The best things to do for the truck stop would be to stock bottled water and to have a back up power supply for electricity. That would be easy to do and would guarantee her steady business for the winter season when the truckers could be stranded. Bonnie was going to keep trying to create social change. Maybe the other truck stops would put in hot tubs, too, and reduce the price of showers for the truckers. But for now, she was tired and just wanted to go home to relax after finding a few good places for her truck stops.

Bonnie was driving along I64, back to home, when the construction work started to seriously slow down the trip with the stopped jumble of cars. She pulled off on the next exit so that she could drive the back roads through the farm country. Most people would be afraid of this at night. The area was isolated and full of wolves. In the winter, the wolves would come closer, drawn to the bright lights in the areas where the people lived. Night jogging in eastern Kentucky cities was not popular because the wolves could just walk through the towns.

She spotted lights just up ahead. Turning off her headlights, she drove slowly to a pull off spot. She walked gingerly to see what was happening. Many people were gagged and tied up, captive on the ground. Some other people were stepping on their throats, using their shoe to hold the heads of the captives steady so that they could brand an "L" on their frightened faces. Bonnie could guess that the "L" was for Louisville, where the great mafia takeover had pushed the landowners off of their property and had impoverished thousands of people. The "L" would be seen by nobody else because the bodies would disappear. Those were the soon-to-be-dead picks from Louisville. The invaders, the illegal narcotics dealers, that had trained at drug meets, to learn how to rob, swindle, and murder.

She did not turn into a pillar of salt because she had watched those picks being destroyed, like the modern day genocide of a Biblical Sodom and Gomorrah culture. Quietly, she walked back to her car. The police had put in the drugs and given the mafia control of each company in Kentucky. The cops wanted everybody to join the pick so that they would have to pay the dope protection money. Then, the picks were treated like ground hamburger. The police would lock up who they wanted and torture who they wanted. Many people had just joined the pick to be safe. But, it was only a cycle of abuse. A no win situation with a gang of thieves.

A society would only progress, with people advancing to a better way of life, if there were helpful individuals in a nurturing environment without thieves. Her life and her people had been ruined by the dope gangs. The truckers had yelled in protest of the mafia takeover, when they had driven through Louisville, Kentucky. The drivers had changed their routes so that they could drive through the city and scream, "We truck, Louisville." They wanted the city streets to run red with the blood of the drug dealing invaders.

She took a sip of buttermilk, ate a bite of catfish with cornbread, and then drove on. Bonnie was cold in the freezing weather and wanted to get home to Carl Silas and warmth. Her husband had brought safety to her world after so much terror. But, Bonnie wondered each day how the dope dealers might be ruining somebody's life.

Leo called her early the next morning. He said, "They really tore up Louisville last night, Bonnie. I heard that they went after the businesses like a quiet riot group. They smashed buildings, smashed equipment, knocked over everything. And all that was done very quietly. We truck, Louisville."

"I thought about you last night when I was looking over some spots to build a truck stop with a free hot tub for the truckers. Louisville started it with their slime dirt county attorney and filth eating police department. I was robbed everyday in that city," Bonnie said.

"What do we think that we should do now, so that we can grow? I like the capsule news report," Leo told her.

"The idea is that if we make a change for the better, then the other companies will copy us. That is how we make overall improvements. Louisville made a change for the worse. So, we push Louisville out."

"We can never push the mafia back out of that city."

"What we can do is to keep the mafia from controlling other cities and not to do business with them while we operate with better services and lower prices," Bonnie said.

"I like the hot tubs. I like your ideas."

"I have to be rich enough to make them work."

"There is one more thing. Mindy had been hanging around the property. I did not even know that it was her. She had actually come inside the office a couple of times asking to talk to a sales person. Her hair was dyed black. She is on the video surveillance recording," Leo told Bonnie.

"What did Mindy do? She will steal anything."

"Well one of the drivers finally recognized her and ran outside saying that she had broken into his car. Then the whole group started yelling that Mindy was in the building trying to kill everybody. So Mindy tried to run out of room and tripped over a desk. She fell face down on the floor and crawled a little until she stood up. Then, she ran to her car, drove off the lot, and hit a pickup truck before she smashed into a building. She was crushed. What do we do? She is dead. Was she married to somebody?" Leo asked.

"We do nothing. She was probably high on dope. And, she has tried to kill me for a life insurance policy in the past. I would never go to her funeral anyway," Bonnie said.

"Okay. That was your sister, not mine. I will keep you posted. We truck, Louisville," he told her and hung up the phone.

Bonnie thought about all the people that had been ruined by the dope gangs. People had been wiped out without any future. Mostly the poor wanted to be in the dope gangs, while the rich fought off the thieves and moved away from the dope. She did not want her kids to be playing in neighborhoods filled with drug dealers.

Earl Mait, Jefferson County Attorney had set up the drug territories. He was a heavy smoker that liked to belittle everybody. Mait went to Our Lady of the Roses Catholic Church on Sunday mornings as part of his political gambit to secure his office as an elected official. He was really just an ugly little person with absolutely nothing but bribe money buying his every decision. Bonnie hated Earl Mait like she hated all dope dealers.

So while Wally Joe and Carl Silas were playing golf on Sunday, Bonnie parked behind a high school football field, near the Our Lady of Roses Church, on a bushy pull off spot that she had hiked through when she was a teenager. She walked toward the church and waited nearby in some trees. Then, she saw what she knew would happen. Earl Mait walked to his car for a cigarette.

She was wearing a red wig, lots of make up to change her face, and dressed in a way that made her look really good. She walked right up to his car and said, "I saw the smoke. Can you give me a cigarette? I left my pack at home."

Mait smiled and said, "Sure. I could not even last through the service without needing to smoke one." He rolled down the car window and held the cigarette pack out for her.

Bonnie leaned in to grab the cigarette. Then she said, "Thanks. We are not supposed to smoke on church property. I am just going to smoke this in the shade of those trees over there."

"Sounds like a good idea. I think that I will follow you," Mait told her.

They walked to the trees without talking. When they were in the shade, Mait said, "It is cooler here."

"Yes. Lots cooler. And something just crawled from your shoulder. I think that you have a spider on the back of your jacket. Let me catch it before it disappears," Bonnie advised him.

She walked behind him and slammed him on the head with a metal pipe. Bonnie continued to pound him after he fell to the ground. Earl Mait was dead when Bonnie left to go back to her car that was hidden in one of her favorite teenage spots. She changed her clothes, wiped off the makeup, took off the wig, and drove home using the back roads.

Bonnie had shrimp and lobster with fresh vegetables ready for Carl Silas when he got home from his golf game. He looked at the food and said, "Do you know that the exercise and heat from playing golf does not make that meal look that good? I just want a salad and a glass of tea."

"We can just put the food in the refrigerator for later. There is a salad right there. The tea is in the kitchen. Would you like some pigs-in-the-blankets?"

"No. Just salad and tea, for now. And, maybe a nap," he said.

"You want to have a nap. And, your all time favorite of pigs-in-the-blankets will not make you happy. Alright. And, I will take a hot bubble bath, while you have a nap, during this unusual change in your habits. Did Kathy play today?"

"Kathy does not know how to play golf."

"Wally Joe said that she was going to use those golf clubs that you gave to me, while he taught her," Bonnie said.

"He never taught her. I think that they broke up, if they were ever actually together."

Bonnie thought to herself, Wally Joe had only called Meredith to see if I went to my office that day, not to ask to borrow golf clubs. That was the way that Mindy had acted when she had stalked Bonnie. Maybe Wally Joe was going to drug meets and planning to wipe them out. Dope dealers did not have any friends because they only hurt people.

Now she was going to have to follow Wally Joe around and check him out, so that she would feel safe again. She could guess, very closely, when he should be at medical school and when he might be somewhere else. He might be stalking her, which would be a big problem for her.

He was like Mindy. And Mindy had been involved in the plot to have Bonnie killed for life insurance. Bonnie had gotten the insurance policy for her parents, so that if she was killed sliding off of a mountain or something, then at least she could smile, knowing that Mom and Dad would be millionaires.

Carl Silas took a shower and went to sleep. Bonnie put the food in the refrigerator and went to get in a hot bubble bath. After three hours of soaking, she went to look for her husband. He was still asleep. And, he was probably not going to get up again until in the morning. He had played golf all day long, in the hot sun, with Wally Joe.

So, Bonnie got out her book on herbs and started to read while she watched her husband sleep. She went to sleep at around one o'clock in the morning. Carl Silas woke up at five o'clock and was ready for breakfast. Bonnie woke up as she heard him opening the closet door.

She asked him, "Are you ready for breakfast?"

"Did I wake you up? Yes, I am ready to eat. But, I think that I want to have some of that shrimp and lobster that I saw last night. You had a whole table full of food. But I was too tired to eat, then. Now, I am starving," her husband told her.

"I am going to get up and fix you something to eat right now. The food is already cooked. So it will warm up really fast. By the time that you have finished shaving, everything should be ready," she said.

"I liked playing golf yesterday. Wally Joe is really good. He had been playing for a long time with those other accountants that he had worked with. I just wanted to keep playing because he seemed to liked being there and playing with me. But, I am starving and my muscles are very sore," he told Bonnie.

She was going to spend some time looking for grass stains on her husband's clothes. Bonnie was going to treat any stains that she found before she washed his clothes. She had seen Carl Silas and Wally Joe wrestle before. And she would guess that if they had spent the whole day together, then they had probably taken a few tumbles on the grass, which would explain why her husband was so tired after riding around on a golf cart.

Bonnie had not been there when Wally Joe had knocked the golf balls off of the golf cart because he had spilled his hot coffee on his shorts when they had hit a bump. The golf balls had went flying everywhere. Carl Silas stopped the golf cart so that he and Wally Joe could pick up the golf balls. Then Wally Joe had made the mistake of throwing a golf ball at Carl Silas. So Carl Silas had retaliated by throwing about five golf balls at Wally Joe.

And when they had finished throwing golf balls at each other, they picked up all the golf balls and put the golf balls back on the golf cart. Then Wally Joe tried to get back on the golf cart and had slipped from the dew on the grass, which made him grab the golf cart to steady himself. The golf cart tilted and Carl Silas was knocked to the ground. And the golf balls fell off of the golf cart again. So then they spent the whole day trying to shove each off of the golf cart while they drove around the golf course. That was why Carl Silas was so tired with aching muscles.

Bonnie only wondered a little what might have happened on the golf course between the Carl Silas and Wally Joe. But she really did not care and was not going to ask Carl Silas any questions about their day of golf. She warmed up the food for Carl Silas, and then went to get dressed. Both of them wanted to get to work early, so she just put the dishes in the dishwasher after they had eaten. She drove to the office and told Meredith that she was going to stay in the office an hour later today. When all the patients had gone for the day, Meredith started cleaning up. And Bonnie waited until Meredith had left the office for the day, before she started checking on the news stories about Earl Mait. The news reporter had written that Earl Mait was missing.

Bonnie wondered if someone had taken Earl Mait's body. They had not been that far from his car, when they had walked into the trees to smoke a cigarette. If people had searched the area, they should have found his body really fast. Those trees were right next to the church parking lot.

She thought about the missing bodies of Brewster and Mait, as she drove away from her office. She did not care who took the bodies. She only wanted to be sure that nobody had seen her and that nobody was following her. Wally Joe had already made her wonder if he was tracking her. She wanted to stay safe and was starting to wish even more that Wally Joe had decided to live somewhere else.

She needed to make one more stop before she went home and started cooking dinner. She had heard about another dope payoff cop. She hit this one hard and the drug cop dropped to the ground. Bonnie hated that maggot like all dope dealers. And, now he was dead.

Then, she heard Wally Joe blurt out, "You just killed that cop. Carl Silas is going to blow a fuse when he hears this."

Wally Joe had probably followed her from her office. She had guessed that he might do that. Then he said, "All you have to do is pay them off Bonnie. They just pick up the bribes so that we can run dope. I just give them a couple of bucks a week."

What Carl Silas was going to blow a fuse about, could be a guess right now. Wally Joe was a dope dealer that was living in her house. She turned slowly to face Wally Joe, like the mist sliding around in a fog. She looked him right in the eye and said, "Did you see him hit me? Why did you just stand there and let him attack me?"

Then she swung the screwdriver that she was holding, into Wally Joe's jaw. She quickly pulled the screwdriver back out, and plunged it into his chest. Now she had to clean up the mess and hide the evidence.

This could be a crime scene where the drug dealer, Wally Joe, kills the payoff cop. The problem with that was that he was still living with them. Bonnie did not need any police problems. His car was parked somewhere. But, Bonnie had her car to take care of, too. She was standing between two bodies and did not want to leave either one of them there.

She decided that the cop's body would stay there. Wally Joe, she could bag up and dump. Carl Silas was going to miss his brother. And, she could have used Wally Joe's spot in medical school. Once she had his body in the car, she would have to drive around to find out where Wally Joe had parked. She had to decide, right now, whether to leave Wally Joe's body or to take it with her. If Wally Joe's body was not found here, then the police would not keep coming back to see Carl Silas with questions.

Luckily, the night was really dark. She could put Wally Joe's body in his car. Taking his wallet and leaving him on the front car seat, he would look like a murder and a robbery victim. That was risky to do. But, it was much better for Bonnie if the bodies were not found together. So she bagged up Wally Joe's body, put it in her car, and went to look for his car.

He had not parked so far away. However, anybody could walk by. Bonnie pulled his body out of her car. Then, she put Wally Joe's body on the front seat of his car. She pulled off the plastic bags and smeared his clothes and the seat with the bloody bags. Then she smiled, as she thought about how to fix this problem fast. She used his phone to call for a tow truck with a deep, heavy voice. The tow truck would pick up his car in less than an hour.

Bonnie drove home slowly. She threw her bloody clothes, the gloves, and the plastic bags in the fireplace. Then she went to take a hot bath. While the hot water was running into the bathtub, she went back to check on the fire. Her clothes were burned away. She added more wood so that the fire would burn bright.

Wally Joe's stuff was all over their house. She was not going to answer the phone if it rang. Bonnie was going to soak in a bubble bath, the way that she always did, until Carl Silas came home from the night classes that he taught at the medical school.

Carl Silas was tired when he came home. He was excited because Wally Joe had bought tickets to a football game. They were going to go and had an extra ticket.

Bonnie smiled and said, "Sounds like fun. Do we take hot chocolate with a thermos? Or, do you think that you want to go to the game with your brother and without me? You can decide. Which is more fun for you?"

Carl Silas smiled and spoke warmly, "All of us. With you and Wally Joe."

She smiled back and said, "Okay." She wondered if the tickets were in Wally Joe's wallet, that she had dumped. Or, would the tickets be found in the car, in Wally Joe's room? Or were the tickets on order? The football game was not going to be fun. She just wanted to go to bed now. But, she curled up in front of the fire for about an hour after she had cooked steaks with baked potatoes for their dinner. Carl Silas made her feel safe and warm. But there were really a lot of problems for her while she stayed in the area.

And now she had to worry about problems from Wally Joe. Without his wallet, it would take a while for Wally Joe to be traced to their address. The tow truck driver should solve that problem. Carl Silas and the tow truck driver were going to have an unpleasant experience that she could not keep from them. Bonnie really did not have any choice in the matter.

Wally Joe had been a drug dealer. He had followed her and stalked her, while he was also swindling other people with his dope gang. Bonnie wanted his body found and buried so that she could get the funeral over with. Wally Joe had made a horrible problem for her. She had no idea what Wally Joe might have done with his dope gang that could endanger her or Carl Silas. There was really nothing else that she could do, but wait for the phone call about Wally Joe, since he had been living with them.

She went to bed, firmly deciding that Carl Silas would answer the phone and the doorbell. Many married people had secrets in their past. But she and Carl Silas, they were gaining secrets in their marriage. Bonnie was trying to feel some kind of hope for them. This marriage was a lot of work. But, Carl Silas was something that she grown used to while talking about having children.

He answered the phone when it rang at three o'clock in the morning. Carl Silas spoke clearly, "Yes. This is Dr. Blake. Is there a problem at the medical school?"

Randy Dwight, with the campus police said, "No, Dr. Blake. We received a call about your brother, Wallace Joseph Blake. Some course materials were found in his car. A tow truck driver called the police when he found Wally Joe in his car. The police opened the car and called us. The tow truck driver had your address. Wally Joe is dead. Apparently, someone robbed him after he had called for a tow. You need to call Detective Harden with the city police. I am sorry for your loss, Dr. Blake."

Carl Silas hung up the phone. He looked at Bonnie with tears in his eyes. Then he whispered, "Wally Joe is dead. What do we do? I need to call the city police."

Bonnie hugged him. She knew that this was not going to be easy. And she promised, "I am here for you Carl Silas. We will do what needs to be done. I am so sorry for you. We need to call your parents and family, too. They will be hurt if you wait until the morning."

Then she just held him. This marriage was not exactly making her uncomfortable, but she could have wished for a better situation. She was going to let Carl Silas pack up Wally Joe's things. She wondered how she would feel when, and if, they did have children. She had killed Wally Joe. And she felt really great about it, too. Carl Silas was never going to know that. Bonnie hated and killed all dope dealers.

Well, some people voted Republican, some people voted Democrat, and some people voted not at all. Her choice was made a long time ago to kill all drug dealers, including Wally Joe. This was her war. Being alone in her war against dope, in her own house, probably made Bonnie feel as lonely as Wally Joe may have felt without having someone to talk to when he was here. But Wally Joe was gone now. And Bonnie was really very happy about Wally Joe's death. However, she was a professional and did not laugh when Carl Silas, with tears in his eyes, had told her that Wally Joe was dead.

Still Bonnie really had absolutely nobody to talk to about any of those things that she had done. If she were on a battleship, she could talk to the other soldiers about how she felt. But, there was just her to remember each of her fights. There were war markers all across the United States to denote places where a battle had been fought in one of the wars. Her battles were private, without markers, but just as glorious to her. She hated and killed all dope dealers. But, people in the future would not know how they had fought to keep the dope dealers out because there no markers showing the story of their battles.

Part of her job also needed to be, to leave the story for the future generations. She had thought about how she should write a book and leave a legacy for their war, as they drove toward Carl Silas Blake's parents home in Paintsville, Kentucky for Wally Joe's funeral. Carl Silas had packed up everything that had belonged to his brother and left all the boxes at his parents home. Bonnie was incredibly quiet during this whole time because Carl Silas never once made a reference to the fact that the dope gangs had caused his brother's death.

Wally Joe and Bonnie had simply been on opposite sides of a war. And if there were not dope gangs, then Wally Joe would not have been a dope dealer. But mostly, she and Carl Silas had strangely always avoided the conversation about crime and dope gangs. She had told him that she had been terrorized by drug dealers. And, he had told her that she would be safe and free from that terror in his home, as his wife. And, she had been safe.

When they went from the cemetery to his dad's house, Carl Silas told her a little about his childhood. Paintsville was small and safe when he was a child. But because most of the people were so incredibly poor, he really hated the city. He knew when he was a child that he was going to move away from this small town. His family was not poor. But the area was just too isolated for him. Most of the roads were still not paved. And, those dirt roads were just mud and slush in the winter. The whole city was a depressing place with all the poverty, ignorance, and lack of improvements.

Bonnie thought that some people might find the city quiet and quaint. But those people would also have to enjoy being isolated without all the modern conveniences. And, power outages were common in Paintsville. His parents had a auxiliary generator, so that they would always have hot water and electricity. But, most of the people in the town just did not have so many things. And they did not care that they did not have those things. That was the part that Carl Silas like to call ignorance.

She could understand how he would hate to be so isolated with so many very stupid people. He was fastidious and liked to teach. Her husband greatly valued education and technological advancements. And he probably did feel very alone while he was growing up. He may have been the only person here, except for his parents that liked to dream about the future. His mother was a college educated author. And his father was a physician that liked to do medical research.

His parents traveled a lot. So there were many things for them to see without becoming bored from living in tiny Paintsville. And, they were mostly safe living in the small town without many people to bother them. They liked the isolation. But Carl Silas just wanted to leave, as soon as he and Bonnie had arrived. He even said that the boredom would not bother Wally Joe now. They had both hated Paintsville.

Luckily, this was going to be their last day here. They had gone to check Wally Joe's grave at the cemetery so that they could tell his parents that everything was fine. Bonnie shopped quickly at the grocery while her husband waited in the car. Then she took the groceries into the kitchen and started cooking. She had a turkey, a roast, and a ham cooking while she went about cleaning the house. Bonnie scrubbed the bathroom one more time. Then, she put some potatoes in the new microwave that Carl Silas had bought for the kitchen. Her husband was spoiled and did not want to wait very long for hot food. His mom had put the other microwave in her writing studio. So he had bought a microwave for the kitchen.

Once she thought that she had everything organized, she went out to sweep off the front porch. Carl Silas was cleaning up the yard. He saw her and said, "It rained yesterday. And the grass has really grown over night. I really should cut the grass before I leave. And, I noticed that the gutters need to be cleaned. Dad is not going to feel like doing much of anything right now. And way out here, nobody is going to notice if they let the yard go wild for a little while. But, I really should do those things before we go."

"I cleaned the house again. I put more food in the oven. After I changed the linens on our bed, I noticed that there was not very much laundry. Do you want me to do the wash? I can just toss in a few loads. And if you bring out the ladder, I will clean the gutters myself, while you cut the grass. It does not matter what time we leave today? In fact, we can stay very late if you want," she smiled and told her husband.

"Sounds good. And, we are just talking about a few hours of work. My mom likes you. She said that you were beautiful and that I was just afraid that you would get away, so I married you quickly. She is not talking much. That is how I know that she is very upset. And she is afraid for us, because we live in the same city where Wally Joe was killed," he told Bonnie.

"We are very careful, Carl Silas. And, we have lived there for years."

"But, we both work nights. Mom wants us to move to here."

"Here. We can not work and live here, Carl Silas. Can we?"

"No. I hate this city. But, we should be more careful when we get home. Maybe the killer knows about us."

"The killer probably does not even know who we are. Anyway, I run marathons and stay athletic. I can defend myself. You could have the campus police escort you to your car, if you like," Bonnie said. She really did not want to talk about Wally Joe's killer too much, because she had killed Wally Joe. And she was very happy to have killed him.

"No. I am worried about you. I would be very lonely without you. Do you think that you have any ideas about what happened to Wally Joe?" Carl Silas asked her.

Bonnie got cold chills down her spine when he said that. It was like she had been expecting that question for a long time. And, not just about Wally Joe's murder. If wally Joe was having his dope dealers call and tell him where she went, then she might have a big problem. She did not want to attract attention. And, she did not know how big his gang might be. Bonnie needed to think about how to change the things that she did in her war so that she would not get caught.

"Carl Silas, I just think that somebody had the advantage. I have had to fight people off in the past. I had more than a few bad times with rough people when I was driving a truck. I always watch my back. Maybe, because Wally Joe was so tall, he thought that nobody would challenge him. You have to carry yourself in a way to prevent attacks, too," Bonnie said.

"I just can not believe that this has happened," Carl Silas whispered.

"Our kids will have to be protected, too," she told him while she was trying to change the subject.

Carl Silas wanted kids. And, she knew that they were going to be safe from Wally Joe's attacker because she had killed Wally Joe. So she just wanted to get everything done and leave, without anymore talk about the killer, because she was already tired. Everyone had been talking about the killer for days. And, she already knew that they were never going to catch the person that had murdered Wally Joe. She only wanted to kill him again.

They hugged and kissed his parents as they left. When they were driving back, Bonnie got out the snacks. Then she said, "Are we going straight home? I thought that maybe you could show me some of those scenic drives in this moonlight."

"I know a few nice roads. We will take a little scenic tour on the way back. Can I have some iced tea?" her husband asked.

She handed him the tea as she said, "Here is the tea. And, I will put the snacks on the armrest. I am going to put my feet up."

They drove through miles of country back roads. After about a hour, they saw some lights in a clearing up ahead. Carl Silas stopped the car and said, "That looks suspicious way out here. Do you think that we should investigate?"

"You do not live around here anymore, Carl Silas. And, remember what happened to Wally Joe. That is private land. I think that we should mind our own business, which is many miles away at our home. The drive was nice. But, maybe we should just head home."

"I just wanted to know if that was a problem. We can go straight home, if you want."

"I do want to go home. I have almost eaten all of the snacks. And we have a refrigerator full of food at home. I do not think that is a problem up ahead. Probably just a bonfire. And, none of our business," she told her husband.

Bonnie spent a lot time adjusting the music while they drove past the illuminated area so that she could distract her husband's attention. That light could be her war. And, she did not want Carl Silas anywhere near her people and their battles. Bonnie would be forced to choose between her war and her husband. And, Bonnie killed all dope dealers with great pleasure. Carl Silas would be in great danger from her if he challenged her war.

She had enjoyed spending time with his parents while they had stayed in Paintsville. Wally Joe's funeral had mostly been about her being introduced to lots of her husband's relatives. She had acted like the perfect hostess and watched out for anything that his parents might need. She was not sad like the rest of the people at the funeral, because she had killed Wally Joe. So, she could concentrate on organizing things for her husband. And she was glad that Carl Silas had never before wanted to spend anytime with his parents in Paintsville. The small town did not have all the luxuries that Bonnie liked to enjoy.

Chapter 7   Future Plans

The next week, Bonnie decided to find some more offices in Atlanta, Georgia. She really wanted to promote the evening office hours for dentists. And Atlanta was a big market and a great place to push her idea forward. She and Carl Silas were talking more and more about children since Wally Joe's death. Her husband really wanted those kids. But, Bonnie needed to have more income coming in, if she was going to have kids. She had to be a millionaire. Then she had to be a billionaire. That was the other way to fight her war.

She had to have better companies and more companies than the dope dealers. And, having her kids was going to slow her down. She was going to have to take care of them and to think of new ways to fight her war. And, she had to be prepared in case Carl Silas ever left her. So she needed more investments that she could trust, like more dentist offices and trucking companies. And her investments would be all hers, until she and her husband decided how to manage their business affairs.

Bonnie wanted to be fair about everything. Carl Silas had brought her to a new high when he had married her. He had given her the time and the opportunity to go to dental school. That was worth something to her. And she did not forget that. But now, that she was making more money from her businesses, she needed to invest her profits and not jeopardize the stability of her companies. The whole reason that she felt safe was because she had Carl Silas to rely on. So he really should share in her profits when she expanded her business. But she would be the one that would take the investment risks with her companies.

He had been even more intense at Wally Joe's funeral because his brother was so young. Everyone had been expecting Wally Joe to graduate from medical school in just a few years and not to suddenly die. And his death was not even accidental, like a car crash. He had been murdered. So Carl Silas, a person that sees death everyday, was completely shocked by everything surrounding Wally Joe's death. And Carl Silas wondered why she was not showing an intense strain, also.

Her husband had reasoned that she taken care of Wally Joe and should have been attached to him. Even though she had only met Wally Joe a few months before, Carl Silas really expected her to be completely frightened and broken apart by his death. He asked her if she still resented the fact that Wally Joe had kissed her in the kitchen when he had came to get some turkey that one night.

Bonnie had told her husband, "There are things to be done now. I am sorry that your brother is dead. I know that you only had one brother. He lived with us. And, I do miss him. But, I was terrorized by thieves. I have learned to channel my feelings in a different way. At least I am able to help your mother and father now. Neither one of them expected to lose a child. They live in this tiny town, away from many things. We should ask them to come and stay with us so that we can care for them. I have an office where I work. I really can not stay here and take care of them. We could take a family leave. But, I am self-employed and you work for a hospital. Do you want me to leave you and care for your parents? Your parents said that they wanted to stay here, and that they would call us if they needed us."

Carl Silas had replied, "We can wait and see how things go with them. I would hate living here, again. This whole city is too boring. And, my parents will not come to live with us unless things get really bad here. We can just check on them. I do need to protect them. Now, there is only me to take of them."

"There is me, too, Carl Silas. But just because your mom likes me, does not mean that I am not a stranger to her. We have never lived in their home as a couple before. Just think about it. She is under a strain just be nice to me. I am really a stranger to her. She needs to be alone so that she can relax," Bonnie said.

"We are going to call and leave messages everyday until I feel safe about them."

"We will check on them everyday. And I will leave messages, too. But, we do need to go home. I need to take care of you, too. This pain does not heal. This pain with mourning just stays with you," Bonnie advised her husband.

When they had gotten home, Carl Silas only took the next day off to sort out things. Then, he went back to work at the hospital because he was not really going to accomplish anything by staying home. He spent most of that one day off by talking to her, telling her about things. Bonnie had to listen about Wally Joe's funeral over and over again. And he talked about Paintsville, which should not have taken very long at all because there is absolutely nothing in Paintsville worth talking about. Bonnie was quite sure that one of the fun things to do in Paintsville was to watch your eyebrows grow. The town was so tiny, that even if every one of the residents were at home, you would still feel isolated, like being the only one living on a mountain top.

And during their talks, Carl Silas was just waiting for her to crumble because Wally Joe was dead. The only thing that Bonnie wanted to do about Wally Joe was to spit on him while he was in his coffin. Her husband's parents would have been greatly shocked by that. She thought about putting her finger in her eye, so that her eye would tear up. But she had changed her mind, because Carl Silas was so upset, that he was not really going to notice if she did not cry at the funeral. But, she would be in big trouble, if she did spit on Wally Joe while he was in the coffin. So she was not going to spit on him and not going to cry.

Then after they been back home for a few days following the funeral, Carl Silas had walked in to tell her the news about the University of Kentucky. And, he was correct about all of that abuse. The students were being expelled because of false complaints from the dope dealers that ran the entire campus. The dope dealers would file false complaints. Then the dope dealing U of K staff would push the false complaints through and falsely expel the students. That was the way that gangsters ran a university campus.

Those students came to the University of Kentucky to get a degree, not to be terrorized by gangsters. U of K had advertisements all over the state to attract the new students. The U of K ads would spotlight the university as a nice place. Most of the new students did not even have any friends on campus. They would come to U of K and get abused by the staff. And the students could not complain to anyone. The campus was run by gangsters. And gangsters only rob people, not handle complaints.

Bonnie already knew that the area was really bad. They just did not see all the problems because they lived in a big house with lots of security. The gate to their property kept the thieves out. But their kids would have to socialize with other kids in that same area. Bonnie could not really see any point in having children and being forced to send them away to a boarding school for their safety. She would need to protect her kids and to watch them grow. Her fortune was going to be for her kids in the future.

And now the only places that she would go were to her office and to shop in the stores. She had no idea how close Wally Joe's dope gang might be to her. She could not risk being caught killing a dope dealer. And she was still curious about how some of the bodies had disappeared. The news stories had reported that Earl Mait, the Jefferson County Attorney, had disappeared. And Brewster was reported as missing. So Bonnie knew that something was happening. She just did not know what. And she did not want to know, either. It really was good enough that they were both dead without any explanation about the bodies. Because Bonnie did kill all dope dealers, she was just happy that they were dead.

But Wally Joe had shown up right behind her, after she had killed that other dope payoff cop. She could almost feel that someone had called Wally Joe and told him where she was. But he had acted so quickly, that she had been forced to kill him before he could tell her if anybody had called him. He had said that Carl Silas was going to be upset because she had killed a cop. And her trigger had snapped. So she had killed him. But she had really wanted to know if he had been called by a dope dealer. That had made her do something that she had never done before when she had killed a dope dealer. She had hidden Wally Joe's phone in her things.

She would have preferred not to have had his phone. But since he was her brother-in-law, she could always say that he given it to her, or had left it with her. She had all the information from the phone and just needed to research the numbers. But Carl Silas had been spending so much time with her since Wally Joe had died, that she had not had much time to check out the phone information. Wally Joe had received a call on that phone before he had spoken to her that day. But, she still could not understand why he had talked to her after he had watched her kill that cop.

Maybe Wally Joe had just been following her. Either way, he saw her kill a cop. So she had to kill him. But then again, he was a dope dealer. So he had probably killed people, too. He had just stood there and calmly talked to her. Carl Silas was the one that Wally Joe had thought was going to be upset by the murder. Now she had to find out who had called Wally Joe because that person may know something about her that could get her into a lot of trouble.

Bonnie used a public phone to call the number. A woman answered the phone. Then Bonnie had hung up the phone. She needed to know who that woman was, needed to know her name. But, the voice had sounded so familiar. So Bonnie had panicked and hung up the phone. She waited an hour, then called the number again. That time she got the answering machine with the message, "Hi. This is Page. Just leave a message." Page had sounded like Page Hempson, Beth's mother. That was why the voice had been so familiar. Bonnie was used to hearing that voice while it was yelling.

Page would always come home from work and start yelling. Since Bonnie had been taking care of her own home, she was always confused as to why Page Hempson could not keep her own house clean and organized. Her husband James did not even care about their messy house. Page would take forever to do anything. She was the kind of person that could irritate anybody. And now Page had been calling Wally Joe. She might not even know that Wally Joe was dead.

Bonnie found a current address for Page Hempson and called her again on the public phone. This time Page answered the phone. So Bonnie changed her voice and said, "Page Hempson, is that you?"

"Yes, this is Page. Who is this?" Page answered her.

"I have not seen Beth in a long time. Do you know how to find her? I saw James last week. And he said that you would know where Beth was. James told me to call you."

"That is why James moved out of our house. He always tells people to do things like that. He was chasing after one of Beth's girlfriends. That girl is just as old as his daughter. Do you know Bonnie? Well my husband really likes that girl. And he could be her father. I had some people watching him. Then I called Bonnie's brother-in-law to find out what was going on between them. Bonnie is married now. But that will not stop James. Her brother-in-law said that he would follow her and see if she was meeting James. Then Wally Joe did not call me back. He called me one day and told me that Bonnie was leaving her office. I called him back and told him to follow her because James took off from work that same day," Page told her.

"Was Wally Joe in your group?" Bonnie asked Page, in her different voice.

"Everybody is in a group today. Wally Joe and I ran with the same picks. But Bonnie is a dentist, married to a doctor, absolutely gorgeous. And my husband thinks that she would want something to do with him."

"So you are a pick? Did you buy dope from Wally Joe? Or did Wally Joe buy dope from you?"

Page made three taps on the phone and said, "I said that I am a pick. Wally Joe and I just ran with the same picks. I can sell you something. What do you need? Marijuana?"

"No. I was looking for Beth."

"Did she rob you? She has stolen everything from my house."

"Yes. That was it. She robbed me."

"I threw her out a long time ago. She stayed high on dope. I have not seen her in years," Page said.

"Then I will let you go."

"Do you need to buy some?"

"Not now, thanks," Bonnie said in her different voice, as she hung up the phone. That had made her feel safer. But she did not fully believe it. Still nothing else unusual had happened since Wally Joe had died. And like Beth, Page just made a mess of things. Wally Joe was a dope dealer that was sent to his death by Page. And Bonnie had never had any interest in James.

Wally Joe had really scared Bonnie that day. And because he was a dope dealer, he could have killed Bonnie or her husband at any time. So Page had done her a favor in an offbeat sort of way, by sending Wally Joe to Bonnie. Bonnie watched things very closely for about another week. She needed to know that her only threat came from Page.

After a week, nothing unusual had happened. So Bonnie relaxed a little more. Two weeks later she parked near Page's office. She walked into the parking garage and saw Page going toward her car. Bonnie walked past her and then turned around. Page had not looked directly at her. But Page did stop quite suddenly and mutter, "Bonnie. Bonnie. That is Bonnie."

Page turned around and stared at Bonnie. Then she asked, "Bonnie is James with you?"

"Page, James is not with me. James is your husband. Are you alright?" Bonnie asked her.

"I thought that James was with you."

"James is not with me. Is he selling drugs? Somebody told me that. But I did not believe it."

"James does not want to be in the pick. He just left me. We have meetings and everything. You can meet people. "

"You like the meetings?"

"I am selling everything for my group. My marijuana is a special price."

"There is James, over there," Bonnie said as she took the metal pipe out of her pocket. When Page turned to look for James, Bonnie hit her on the head. And then she kept hitting her until she was dead. Then she opened the door to Page's car, and put Page on the front seat. Bonnie locked the car door and left. Then she drove the back roads to get home.

She thought about how Page had told her that James was not selling drugs. She did not really believe anything that Page told her. What Bonnie had wanted to do was to ask Page why she had been calling Bonnie's brother-in-law, Wally Joe. But Page had not acted like she was afraid of Bonnie. So Bonnie had just wanted to keep everything smooth without upsetting Page before she had killed her. Bonnie was watching and listening to Page so that she could learn what Page might know. But, Page had only been asking about James. Bonnie wondered why James had not told her that he had left Page, when Bonnie had last seen him. Maybe, that was because he had never left his wife.

Page was dead now. And Bonnie felt relieved and happy that another dope dealer was gone. When Bonnie had been growing up, Page had always seem to be in the background. They would all watch the television at the Hempson's in peace, until Page came home. Suddenly, Page would walk in the door and complain about everything. Page wanted to know why the house was not cleaned, why the dishes were not washed, and why the laundry was not done. Page had a job and expected the kids to do all the work.

One night Page came in from shopping for new clothes, and asked Bonnie to hem a new pair of pants for her. Page wanted to wear the pants to work the next day. So Bonnie hemmed the slacks in about thirty minutes, by hand, with a needle and thread. Page had bought the new clothes because she had a weight problem and could not fit into any of her dress slacks. She was always griping about everything. And her husband was a flirt that sat around with the kids and listened to her complaints. It was no wonder that her daughter, Beth was such a lousy person.

And Page could have made things really bad for Bonnie if she had talked about her flirting husband, James. Bonnie's parents would have not understood any of that. Bonnie was Catholic just like her parents. Her parents were strict. Bonnie still wondered how her brothers and sisters could be dope dealers when they were all raised by the same parents. Bonnie had always followed her parents decisions and wishes.

She was very respectful of her parents. If her mom had wanted something done, then Bonnie would just do it, no questions asked. She did the same thing for her dad. Bonnie just wanted them to say what they wanted, so that she could get it done. And she was really like that with everybody. She just wanted people to say what they wanted. It was easier than guessing what people wanted you to do for them. Once people had told her what they wanted, she did not have to talk to them anymore. She just needed to do whatever it was that they needed done and then go on about her own business.

That was her special honor for parents. She did what they said without arguing, except when it came to her life. Her life was her life. But, she would do absolutely anything for anyone. So her best friend had become Beth because she needed to have a best friend. And if anyone had asked Bonnie, when she was child, to name the people that she liked, she would not have been able to name anyone, because she did not like anyone. People could really bother Bonnie. So she would find activities for them to do, far away from her.

That was the depressing part of her childhood. She could not wait to grow up and move away from home. Her first night away from home, she sat in her new living room, watching television, drinking hot tea, and eating cheese with crackers. She looked at the boxes that she had to unpack and was happy. That was when Bonnie started her policy of never being at home. She did not answer the door, did not answer the phone, and was always too busy. If you left her a message, she would take care of the problem. But she did not want to talk to you. She did not want to hang out with anybody.

Bonnie would go to Florida every two weeks. She was going to move to Florida after she had finished her college degree, and work in research. Seeing everything and learning about everything was very important to Bonnie. She just believed that if there was a problem, then it should be corrected. She liked to marvel at all the scientific discoveries and research methods. She was so impressed with the cure for polio and the other advances. Louisville, Kentucky had been a place for polio victims to be treated. The disease was so debilitating. One of Bonnie's cousins, Alice had married Sam, a man that had suffered from polio. Sam was crippled and deformed on one side of his body. He wore a suit to work. So you would never even notice the deformity unless you watched him walk. Sam had an uneven gait and would lean toward his crippled side.

She could have done something about those problems if she had been a doctor back then. Bonnie knew that you had to push to accomplish things. After polio became such a huge problem with many victims, then the vaccines were developed. But many people had to die before the IPV, Inactivated Poliovirus Vaccine, and the OPV, Oral Poliovirus Vaccine were found. Now, polio could be cured by swallowing a vaccine or by having a vaccine shot.

Bonnie became really discouraged as she thought about her childhood, during the drive back to her home. Seeing Page again had made all her memories come flooding back to her. She had another cousin, Martin who had married Lisa. His wife was always telling stories about Waverly Hills Sanatorium in Jefferson County. Her mom had come to Louisville because she had tuberculosis. She was treated at Waverly Hills Sanatorium where she died. Because so many people had died there, the sanatorium decided to avoid depressing the patients with so many deaths. So they began sending the bodies out a private tunnel that travelled down the hill. The tunnel had been originally designed so that the workers would not have problems with ice while going up the hill to the sanatorium.

Lisa liked to talked about the Iron Lung that had helped her mother to breathe. She been told over and over about how the negative pressure ventilator, the Iron Long put pressure on her mother's chest so that the air would go in and out of her lungs. Lisa thought that the sanatorium had been a frightening place with all those people dying. She had just wanted her mother to come home instead of being carried down the tunnel with the rest of the dead.

Because of so many deaths, somebody had been forced to correct the problems with polio and tuberculosis. Now Bonnie was trying to stop the dope dealers because of all the lives that had been destroyed. The biggest part of the Louisville trouble was that people had went to the city for help with things like polio and tuberculosis, in the past. The city with the cures had become a dangerous arena for dope dealers and thieves, not competent healthcare. What had been violated was the trust that the people had placed in the city of Louisville.

That had made her worry more about her situation. Bonnie wanted to buy another house in the area just because she wanted to have another house. She really was not sure what to tell Carl Silas, but she knew that she wanted to buy another house. So she was just going to go ahead and buy another house, and tell Carl Silas that the house was for his parents to use so that they would come to visit. Bonnie did not want anymore long time visitors in her home. Wally Joe had just been too much of a threat to her.

The real estate agent met her at the office at five o'clock in the morning because he was going to get a large commission from the sale. Bonnie signed the papers for the house and gave them the check for $400,000. She drove out to the house and walked through it again. Leaving her car in the driveway, she walked a couple of miles to the truck stop. She bought a root beer and waited outside. The Lotus trucker saw her as soon as he drove onto the lot. Jeffrey waved and parked the truck. Bonnie climbed into the cab.

She smiled at Jeffrey and said, "The last time that I was in a truck, we were yelling as we drove through Louisville so that we could push the gangsters out."

"We truck, Louisville," Jeffrey said as he grinned back at Bonnie.

"We yelled until Bert Night went after us for his dope dealers. That whole city turned to nothing but filth," Bonnie said.

"So he went after us for his gangsters. We truck, Louisville, Bonnie, now and forever."

"We still do not have to carry any of their Louisville loads. I do not want my kids terrorized by dope dealers."

"I do not want a Louisville load. I do not want to drive through that city full of dope dealers," Jeffrey said.

"And the University of Kentucky started expelling kids because they will not sell dope. The gangsters that run that campus just file false complaints to get the kids thrown out. Where are you going to send your kids to college, Jeffrey?"

"Do you think a dope dealer killed Wally Joe?"

"The area is too dangerous with drug dealers. We truck, Louisville," Bonnie answered.

"Who is going to pick you up on the way back?"

"I will try to catch a ride with the first Lotus truck that comes back tomorrow."

"Business has picked up for us. It might be me," Jeffrey said.

"I am trying to control the prices. And my drivers do the rest. All the companies have said that they like my drivers. I want all the drivers to be comfortable in the cab. I got the news capsulized report to keep you connected. All the drivers will receive emergency warnings anywhere they are. You will know about floods, tornadoes, and hurricanes. My uncle gave me this company so that I could help you. We have to grow. And we have to fight with and compete against dope dealers," Bonnie told him.

"We were losing money."

"We were losing money because the dope dealers were hitting our trucks, our drivers, and our loads. Now, we do not carry any Louisville loads. We truck, Louisville."

"Why did your uncle really give you the company?" Jeffrey asked her.

"He wanted me to go to medical school."

"Like your husband."

"I am still trying to go to medical school. I just need to send in some more current applications. My work as a dentist will help me because I have a medical background. But really all of the applicants have about the same qualifications. There are just more applicants than openings. And each year, the number of applicants increases," Bonnie said.

"What happens to Lotus trucking, then?"

"Lotus Trucking is mine for always. I am trying to buy some more trucking companies so that we can grow and have more power. We have to do a good job."

"You are not going to live forever, Bonnie."

"I am building an empire for my kids. We have to fight. And I have to have some little fighters to run my companies and compete against lying dope dealers."

"Why are you going to Atlanta?" Jeffrey asked.

"I am looking for branch offices in Atlanta for my dental practice. I want to keep expanding and offering evening appointments. Then my drivers could have free dental care in Atlanta, too."

"Those things help. What about free medical care?"

"My husband is the doctor. The free dental care comes from me. That is just supposed to be an incentive to keep the drivers because we had some problems. I am working on a plan to offer a super discount dental insurance package. My offices have to make money. And just to make things clear. My husband will not offer free medical care. I am trying to make sure that all the drivers earn a super wage, have good benefits, and can afford to buy a good insurance plan," Bonnie said.

"Do you want to drive?"

"I thought that you would never ask. Go and shop, if you want. Then I will pull us out of here," Bonnie said.

When Jeffrey came back, Bonnie took over and headed south. She was quiet for a long time while she was getting used to driving a rig again. Jeffrey kept singing the whole time. Then he started talking about his family. They were going to be about twenty miles from his home, when they dropped their load. Bonnie said that they should stop by his home. They would still have enough time to pick up the next load and haul it, before the delivery date.

She said that Jeffrey should stay the night at his home. Bonnie said that she would deliver the load and go pick up the next one. Then she would pick him up on the way back so that they could go to Atlanta. After she dropped him off, she headed for the delivery point and dropped the load. Then she called her husband.

"Hi, Bonnie. What do you need?" Carl Silas asked her, when he answered the phone.

"I am in Tennessee. I wanted to tell you that I bought a house today for $400, 000, cash," Bonnie said.

"Why are you in Tennessee? Did you leave me?"

"No. I need to look over some offices in Atlanta so that I can expand my dental practice," Bonnie answered.

"Are you going to be very late tonight?"

"I am coming back tomorrow. I just dropped the driver off so that he could spend the night at home."

"You got a driver. And then you drove yourself," Carl Silas said.

"I am in a Lotus truck. Jeffrey wanted to go home. So I said that I would pick up the load."

"Why did this happen now?" Carl Silas asked her.

"I was talking about the offices with the leasing agent. And she told me that someone else wanted to lease the offices tomorrow. I really can not lease anything without seeing the offices. I do not have an agent in Atlanta. So I need to look over the offices and get an agent," Bonnie said.

"How are you going to find an agent?"

"The leasing agent said that she could work for me. But, I wanted to meet her. The problem happened because I let Jeffrey go home. I was going to catch a ride with a truck back to home."

"Why did you buy a house?" Carl Silas asked her.

"The house is for your parents."

"My parents live in Paintsville."

"You hate Paintsville. Now your parents can stay here for the winter."

"You spent $400,000 on my parents," Carl Silas said.

"I like to shop. Besides, I keep worrying about your mom and dad. Now they have a winter home. The money was mine from my dental practice. I have to keep expanding so that I can buy them a yacht," Bonnie said.

"Why an overnight trip?"

"I could not say no. I was talking to a trucker. Mostly, I was joking about coming back tomorrow. And Jeffrey took me seriously. I already miss my bubble bath. I am staying in the truck tonight. I am getting ready to drive to pick up a load," Bonnie said.

"Why did you do this?"

"I would have been home by eleven o'clock tonight. I want your parents to come whenever they want and stay in the new house. Your mother and I are talking everyday, " Bonnie said.

"I do not want to be alone tonight."

"I liked the house. I was having a problem trying to decide what to do with the home. They took $300,000 off of the price because I paid cash. I am expanding my business. The first use that I came up with, was for your parents. It was a quick sale from the leasing agent. We can always sell the house for full price," Bonnie said.

"We have two homes according to what my wife has just told me. Then you tell me that you are sleeping in a truck at some company in Tennessee," Carl Silas said.

"Yes. Carl Silas, that is correct. That is why I need an agent. I need to be incorporated."

"Right now I would not care if Jeffrey was your agent. I want you to stay home with me."

"I want to stay home, too. Do you want me to come back? I can just catch a ride on the next Lotus truck that comes through. I really need to keep up with the trucking company, too. And I wanted to drive. That will mean that I do not get my agent or those offices in Atlanta," Bonnie said.

"Will you call me again in twenty minutes when you have figured a way around this? You do tend to solve problems fast. I want you home tonight."

"I will call and think of a solution," Bonnie promised her husband.

So Bonnie started to think of a solution. The first thing was that Jeffrey was still going to stay home tonight. Carl Silas would put Jeffrey back in the truck. She was going for a solution that kept Jeffrey at home tonight. Bonnie had really just wanted to drive the rig for awhile.

Then she called the Atlanta leasing agent that was also an attorney. She said that she wanted to see her and the property after three o'clock today. Then she called her dispatcher, Russell, and asked for a Lotus team that might be coming her way. He told her that she already had a team that was waiting for a load about fifteen miles away.

"Is there a problem, Bonnie?" Russell asked her.

"I just need to be home tonight. Change of plans," Bonnie said.

"Do you want Jeffrey to come back?" Russell asked her.

"No. I said that Jeffrey could stay home tonight. I want one of the team drivers to stay with this truck. Can you get me to Atlanta?"

"I have a truck that can pick you up in about thirty minutes," Russell told her.

"Good. Now route me back home for tonight."

"I will have a driver wait at the Atlanta hub until you are ready to leave," Russell said.

"Good plan. We just spent a little more gas than usual. But my driver is home tonight. We should try to work on nights at home for drivers when the shipping points are close to home. See what you can come up with. I will have a few plans ready for a tomorrow afternoon conference call with you. Thanks, Russell," Bonnie said.

Then Bonnie called the team drivers, Tom and Albert. She said "Hi, Albert. Hi, Tom. I let Jeffrey go home tonight. I was going to watch the truck for him. Now, I need to go home. I need one of you to stay with this truck. Who wants to watch this truck and pick up Jeffrey tomorrow? I told dispatch that we are going to try to let the drivers go home when the shipping points are close to home."

"We are coming, Bonnie. We should be there in about twenty-five minutes," Albert told her and hung up the phone.

Tom and Albert arrived later than the Lotus truck that was going to take her to Atlanta. Bonnie was talking to her driver, Clarence, when the team arrived. Tom and Albert raced over to Bonnie to find out what had happened.

"What is the problem, Bonnie? We truck, Louisville. Did they hit?" Albert asked her.

"No. Albert, I just need to get home. My husband is not a trucker. He is a doctor. And things happen. I really just wanted to drive the rig for awhile so that I could keep in contact with you guys. I may start calling each one of you twice a week to ask about any problems. This is a rough job. And I know it. Now I have to leave with Clarence. We truck, Louisville. Be careful, Tom and Albert," Bonnie said.

She told Clarence to wait for a few minutes while she made a phone call. Bonnie called her husband. She was really pumped up from talking to the drivers. Bonnie started laughing and said, "Carl Silas, I called you with the first plan. Now I am routed back to home for tonight. I come back with a driver from the Atlanta Lotus hub."

"Why are laughing? You spent $400,000 today," he replied very seriously to her.

"I bought a $700,000 home for $400,000. The house is actually worth more than that. But the property has been on the market for more than a year. I just liked the house. And I did want to talk to my drivers today," Bonnie said.

"And you will be home tonight?"

"Yes. I will be home to cook your dinner. The Atlanta leasing agent is an attorney. I can see the property and think about the deal on the way back home. I should not be in Atlanta for more than an hour," Bonnie said.

"How did you do it? I really thought that you would be gone tonight."

"I just brought over one of the drivers from a team to watch the truck. And Jeffrey gets to stay home tonight. The shipping point was close to his home. And I did not tell the drivers that I had to be home in time to cook dinner for my husband. Like I said, I had just called to ask your opinion and to tell you what was going on. I really love my drivers and my husband," Bonnie said.

"Now I am happy again," Carl Silas told her. "And, I called your mom to tell her about the house. It really was a good deal. I just was not able to jump from the deal, to the good use for the house. If we hold it for a $700,000 sale price, we would make enough for almost two more Peterbilts. I do want to be a millionaire. And I do want to make you happy. I love you," Bonnie said.

"Mom called me, too. She said that they might stay in the house for a month after next week."

"Good. And not a problem. I just need to make more money than I spend. Today, I spent a lot. But, your parents are priceless. This Atlanta agent may be able to help me with the Lotus hub. I just need a representative in the area. I will probably be home about thiry minutes after you. This makes me want to buy a plane. I have taken flying lessons," Bonnie said.

"I just want you home."

"I am going to write down that priority. I will be home each night, to stay with my husband. I do love you. Now I have to go, so that I can get home tonight," Bonnie said as she hung up the phone.

Bonnie talked to the agent in Atlanta and looked over the property for about forty-five minutes. She told the agent that she would contact her before the office opened again in the morning. Then she started walking toward the Lotus hub. Bonnie saw a Lotus truck parked on the parking lot next to the office building. The driver waved to her. Bonnie walked to the truck and got in the cab. The driver pulled onto the street. And Bonnie was headed back toward home.

"Do we need to stop, Bonnie?" Frank asked her as he drove down the street.

"No, Frank. Now I just go home. Do you need to stop somewhere?"

"Yes. I need to stop at home. My shipping point is close."

Bonnie laughed and said, "I know that the drivers want more home time. This is a rough job with emotional pains. And Jeffrey is staying home tonight."

"Did something happen? Did they hit? We truck, Louisville," Frank said.

"No. I need to have more offices for dentists so that we can buy more trucking companies. We truck, Louisville. We need to be bigger, so that we can compete more with those filthy dope dealers. And I want to finalize a plan for the drivers, with nights at home, for close shipping points," Bonnie said.

Bonnie got home before Carl Silas did. She had dinner in the oven when he walked through the door. He just stood there and stared at her. He was very serious when he said, "Did you really buy a house today? Did you go to Atlanta? How did you get home before I did?"

"I would just give the house to your mom and dad if I thought that they would visit more. I was in Atlanta for more than thirty minutes, today. I wanted to hurry home so that I could cook your dinner," Bonnie told him.

"Not a joke?" Carl Silas asked.

"I never joke, Carl Silas. We truck.... I mean, what I mean is, I need to be a millionaire. And I need to be home with you. So I am going to do both," Bonnie said.

"Why a millionaire?"

"So we can leave companies to our kids. To make the world a better place with recycling and efficient management."

"You can do this? Be home with me and be happy?" Carl Silas asked her.

"Carl Silas, I do not want to leave you. Trucking is a rough job. Instead of sleeping in the sleeper in my Peterbilt, I am going to take a hot bath tonight. I am trying to make truck drivers happier with their jobs. They do not go home every night. I have a responsibility to my drivers. And now, I have a local attorney in Atlanta to represent me when I need help. I need to staff my offices with dentists," Bonnie told him.

"This will make you happy?"

"I do not like all the problems in the world. I am in a position to make a change. If I operate a good company, then I will provide a good service. I can push out the bad companies. I can make a difference. I have been running things with my computer anyway. And I do feel very strongly about evening and weekend office hours for dentists. That gives me lots of early morning free time. All that really happened to you today, Carl Silas, was phone calls. I was home before you were," Bonnie said.

"True enough," her husband replied to her.

Then he hugged her and kissed her, before he sat down for dinner. She was quiet while they ate because she wanted business conversations to stay in her office. They walked upstairs to go to sleep and held hands the whole way. Bonnie thought that they would probably have kids in the next few years. She needed to watch her businesses so that she could turn a profit and fight dope dealers. And she needed to take care of her husband so that he would always be there when she got home from her battles.

The years would be longer for Bonnie with her war. But she would not be able to go to sleep at all if she did nothing about the gangsters. She was always thinking about who the dope dealers might be hurting and might be killing. Somebody had fought against polio and tuberculosis because they knew how to fight against a disease. Bonnie knew how to fight against dope dealers. She just killed them. She just killed all dope dealers like any deadly disease.

Carl Silas was quietly sleeping when she went to bed. He wanted her to be home tonight, so she came back home. Her husband would keep her safe and warm if her investments fell through. She could not really tell her truckers that she had to come back home so that her husband would not be alone tonight. The truckers stayed on the road and hardly ever saw their families. They helped Lotus Trucking, so she helped her truckers. And they had fought so hard to push the mafia back out of Louisville, Kentucky. Now she was asking her drivers to shave their armpits so that they would not offend the clients.

When she woke up, Carl Silas was already up and out of the bedroom. Bonnie got up and went to find him. He was sitting at the kitchen table, drinking coffee and reading the paperwork that she had left there last night. He was wearing a sleeveless shirt with his shorts. His hair was still wet from his shower. The clock was only showing five o'clock in the morning, but Bonnie felt like she was late because Carl Silas was already up.

Bonnie said, "Do want me to make breakfast now? I was really tired from yesterday. You never wake up before I do. And, I was sleeping in our bed last night instead of my truck, because of you."

"Your driver was probably very happy to be at home last night. I was just reading these notes for your drivers. They get daily news reports," Carl Silas said.

"When the Trade Towers were bombed in New York, most of the truckers did not even know what had happened until many hours later. I want the cabs to be like an office for them. Trucking is a very rough job. And, I need to keep my truckers for my company," Bonnie told him.

Carl Silas asked her, "How could you, with all your bubble baths, possibly have survived while driving a truck?"

"I am a trucker. I believe in the trucking industry."

"I married a trucker, too."

"You already knew that you had married a trucker."

"Yes, but I did not know all the rules."

"Every business has guidelines. I am going to make some hot tea. Can I make you something now?" she ask him.

"Breakfast. I am ready for breakfast," he said. Then he walked over to the cabinet and got a glass for his orange juice. When he raised his arm, Bonnie noticed that he had shaved his armpit.

"You shaved your armpit. I always snuggle up to your side so that I can stay warm," Bonnie said.

"I read your memo about shaving that was for your drivers. I think that this will be a cleaner look for the golf course," he told her.

"You know that you can also peel away the dead skin that builds up with the daily use of a deodorant."

"I am just going to try this for awhile, until I decide how I like it," he told her.

So Carl Silas was going to try something new. She wanted all her truckers to do it. But she could only ask them if they wanted to do it. She had to protect them and her company at the same time. Lotus Trucking had to keep growing so that she could fight the dope dealers. Her people were warriors that had to stay well groomed so that they could compete in the business world. And while they were working on their personal hygiene, Bonnie would always be thinking about the kids that were being terrorized by the gangs. Bonnie was a Louisville Exile and knew all about the terror.

She knew that she wanted to be a millionaire, so that she could fight dope dealers. But, Carl Silas only knew that she wanted to compete against the corrupt companies. He had shaved his armpits after he had read her posted memo that was for her drivers. He wanted to bond a little more with her businesses. But there would always be a void between them, because Bonnie did hate and kill all drug dealers. And now, she was ready to fight them on a larger scale, business to business. Because Bonnie and her companies would always reflect the goals of the truckers when they had yelled, "We truck, Louisville."

The End We Truck Louisville. Beverly Feathers. All Rights Reserved. Email: beverlyfeathers@aol.com